"The man's impossible."

Laura Cresswood said nothing as the supervisory nurse, Sylvia Summers, continued. "He wants everything his way, including the exact timing of our visits—which is impossible to predict. Why he chooses to live up there on that mountain—"

"Especially with all that money," one of the field nurses interrupted as she scooted past Laura's desk.

"The man is a hermit," Sylvia continued. "And he's already run off two physical therapists." She handed the chart to Laura. "Now it's your turn. The chart should be labeled P.I.A., because the guy's a genuine pain in the—"

"I've handled P.I.A.'s before," Laura answered quietly. *And I'm an expert on rich, demanding men.*

"This is a really tough case, Laura. No one wants to deal with Adam Scott, much less stay on that mountain to give him his therapy."

"You told me all that, and about the car accident." Laura flipped back a page in the chart. "It says here he's a widower. Was his wife killed in the crash?"

"Yes." Sylvia ran a hand through her short-cropped hair. "A terrible accident. You know, since you're taking this on as a private contract, you'll be totally on your own. You're a brave woman, Laura."

Bravery has nothing to do with it, Laura thought as she closed the chart.

Dear Reader,

Have you ever noticed how, when your heart is troubled, it helps to go someplace quiet? We all have peaceful spots where we retreat when we need a moment of refuge. Mine is a small duck pond a few blocks from my home. I walk over there and stand on a small arched stone bridge. After a while, the sounds of the ducks quacking and the wind in the cypress trees and the gurgle of the low waterfall soothe my spirit.

But sometimes there are circumstances in life when we need a greater escape, times we need a special, remote place where we can go to experience...a healing. I've had such times myself, and I know firsthand the magical restorative powers of the vast national forests in the mountains of northwestern Montana. The primitive cabin in this story is very much like a real cabin in the Kootenai National Forest where I stayed with some friends many years ago. After I experienced the profound peace and beauty and wholeness of that wilderness, I knew I would use it as a setting in a story some day.

And though Laura Duncan and Adam Scott have retreated to the Montana high country for completely different reasons, it doesn't matter what heartaches drew them there. What matters is their healing. What matters is that in the midst of that wildness and isolation, they find peace...and, more important, they find each other.

Darlene Graham

Your kind comments about my books are always very much appreciated. Visit my web site at http://www.superauthors.com or write to me at P.O. Box 720224, Norman, OK 73070.

UNDER MONTANA SKIES

Darlene Graham

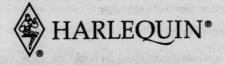

HARLEQUIN®

TORONTO • NEW YORK • LONDON
AMSTERDAM • PARIS • SYDNEY • HAMBURG
STOCKHOLM • ATHENS • TOKYO • MILAN • MADRID
PRAGUE • WARSAW • BUDAPEST • AUCKLAND

ISBN 0-373-70904-8

UNDER MONTANA SKIES

Visit us at www.romance.net

Printed in U.S.A.

This book is dedicated to Marilyn Watley.
Thank you, dearest friend, for taking me to high places.

PROLOGUE

WAS THIS WRONG?

Her conscience squirmed, but Laura Duncan Crestwood reminded herself that she intended to pay Stuart back, even if it took her ten years. She refused to think of herself as the kind of woman who would actually steal.

In fact, she reminded herself and raised her chin, she was a *nice* woman. The kind of woman who complimented the chubby grocery sacker on his new jacket, listened to the elderly lady's third repetition of an old story and smiled at every single baby she encountered, homely or not. A *nice* woman—who was robbing her soon-to-be ex-husband blind. Her chin lowered and her shoulders slumped.

Was this wrong?

"May I get anything else for you, Mrs. Crestwood?" the fashionable young clerk asked.

"I don't think so." Laura smiled a sad little smile and handed over the platinum charge card, the one embossed with STUART HAYDEN CRESTWOOD.

She sighed, folded her hands on the chest-high mahogany counter and studied the high-priced travel accessories under the glass.

Okay, she admitted, she *was* robbing Stuart blind, and probably deaf and dumb, too, but there seemed to be no alternative.

She watched the clerk scanning tag after tag on the heavy woolen sweaters and sturdy jeans that would serve her well in her new life in Montana. *Stuart will have a fit when he gets these bills. Or a heart attack.*

Well, she didn't want *that* exactly. In fact, Laura wanted Stuart to live on and on. Live on, and be completely miserable with that piglet, Charlene. Laura smiled again, not quite so sadly.

Yeah. Wouldn't it be just lovely if Charlene got fat, and Stuart got fatter? Yeah. Stuart would end up being the absentee father she'd always known he would be, and Charlene would morph into the whiny hag that lurked under that false-eyelashed facade.

A guilty frown replaced Laura's smile. She couldn't really wish for that. Unhappy parents wouldn't be good for a child, and Laura truly loved kids. Unfortunately, nature had denied her the ability to bear one of her own.

And right there in the upscale sportswear shop, Laura's eyes started to mist up. Because that was the reason Stuart was leaving her. At least that was her least-painful theory—that he'd only married her because she was a young sexy aerobics instructor who exuded health and...fertility.

When he discovered she *wasn't* fertile, he'd moved on to the next sweet young thing—Charlene. Charlene, who was destined to be his fourth wife. Charlene, destined—Laura had learned only two days ago—to be the mother of the heir to the Crestwood fortune.

And that fortune, she'd learned later the same day, was now parked nineteen thousand miles off the coast of New Zealand. On the Cook Islands to be exact. In an offshore trust.

"Safeguarded," Stuart had claimed, "from frivolous lawsuits."

Safeguarded from Laura was what he meant. After splitting his assets with two previous wives, Stuart Crestwood the Third was not about to allow another divvying up.

"Fraud," Laura's attorney Irene had said as she studied the documents. "But no way to prove it. 'Spouse of the Settlor'—very clever language." She riffled the thick stack of pages with a thumb. "Your name isn't anywhere in here." Irene propped her elbows on her desk. "Face it,

Laura. You will never get your hands on one penny of that nine million."

Laura sighed, then shielded her eyes with a shaky hand. Alone and poor. Just the way she'd started. "Once, when I'd gotten to feeling so hollow, so dead, in this marriage, I actually asked Stuart for a divorce."

"And?" Irene prompted.

"And he started yelling, saying stuff like, 'You came into this marriage with nothing and, by God, you will leave it with nothing.'"

Irene shook her head and spread her palms over the compelling documents. "Unfortunately that was not an idle threat. It would take an entire law firm working full-time to beat this contract, not to mention your prenuptial agreement. Besides, Stuart keeps several big Dallas firms on retainer. None of them will touch your case. Let's face it—Stuart has arranged things so that you can't get at his assets no matter how costly a lawsuit you launch."

Costly lawsuit? Laura couldn't imagine how she was even going to pay Irene's fee for this one brief consultation. Stuart had made certain he held all the purse strings.

The sportswear clerk coughed and looked at her apologetically. "Sorry this is taking so long, Mrs. Crestwood."

"Don't worry about it." Laura flapped a dismissive hand at the pile. So many clothes! But she knew these things would have to last her a very long time. That was why she was buying the best.

She felt suddenly self-conscious, wondering if the young woman had noticed the tears in her eyes. She turned away, focusing on a nearby mirror, pretending to arrange her masses of blond curls.

How could you have been such a class-A idiot? she asked herself as she studied her reflection. No use mentally kicking herself for the millionth time for getting involved with a cold-hearted creep like Stuart Crestwood. She supposed she'd reaped exactly what she'd sown: all this *stuff* and not one shred of happiness.

When she met Stuart right after Gran had died, she'd naively thought he was the answer to a prayer. A handsome man, that powerful, that rich, interested in her, a girl barely out of her teens, a girl who couldn't stick with anything, a—what had her second stepdad called her?—a dingbat.

Stuart had seemed so perfect, so together. Older. Wiser. Who would have guessed he was such a manipulator? Vicious. Cunning.

Thoughts of the real Stuart brought back the

defiance Laura had felt that day in Irene's office when she'd first gotten the bad news, when she'd first hatched this crazy plan.

She wasn't going to wait for Stuart's precious divorce to go through. She was leaving *him*. Without a trace. No lengthy, fruitless court battle like the other wives had fought. Not for her. All she wanted was a little boost to kickstart her new life, to help finance an education that would allow her to be self-supporting. This time she would create a life that was totally her own, without relying on Prince Charming to save her. Never again would she look to a man for security.

But her hand shook a little as she tucked a strand of fluffy hair behind one ear. She had never lived on her own, and she had never lived anywhere but Texas.

She was about to cry. "I'll take these, too." She added a pair of two-hundred-dollar sunglasses to the pile.

The clerk nodded and gave Laura a thin smile as the machine clicked and whirred obligingly, converting another little chunk of Stuart's money into contraband for Laura's flight to freedom.

"Do come back and see us again soon, Mrs. Crestwood," the girl crooned as she slid the charge slip forward.

For a second, Laura wondered if she would miss that. Being Mrs. Stuart Crestwood, getting that reflected respect clerks showed when she whipped out a platinum card and signed that well-heeled last name, dropping a couple of grand as casually as if she was buying a pack of gum. Would she miss that? Without even checking the total, Laura scrawled *Mrs. Stuart H. Crestwood.*

Undoubtedly, in this radical new life she'd set up for herself, she would miss many things—the glittering social life, reported almost weekly in the *Dallas Morning News*; the mansion in Briarwood; never having to cook, clean or even run her own errands—but Stuart was not one of the things she would miss.

Her best friend, Janie, had urged her to "battle it out in court for any of the SOB's money you can get. After all," Janie had argued, "you're already twenty-eight, honey, and even if you are petite and kind of...voluptuous, you're no supermodel. You know what I mean? What are you going to do if you can't find another man to support you? Spend your life *working?* Can you even imagine yourself being some...some *secretary?*"

Maybe Janie's way was smarter. Maybe even easier. Laura was leaving Dallas unskilled and friendless—the future was so uncertain! But however uncertain, this way felt right to Laura. She would make a new life up north; she had to.

Laura gathered her bags of loot, feeling their weight and another twinge of guilt about the devious way she was doing this.

"Goodbye," she told the clerk, and turned, wrapping her determination around herself like armor.

She'd be fine, somehow. Even if she ended up poor, it would be an honest poverty. Well, she'd make it honest. Eventually.

She crammed the sunglasses, with the tag still dangling from the earpiece, onto her nose, and marched out of the store with her chin up.

All that remained was to park her Mercedes convertible in an inconspicuous space in the crowded Wal-Mart lot, stuff her hair under the nondescript hat she'd just bought and call for a taxi.

Investment account, converted to cash.

Plane ticket, bought under an assumed name.

Mrs. Stuart Hayden Crestwood, vanished into thin air.

CHAPTER ONE

Four years later, fifty miles deep in the remote Kootenai National Forest of northwestern Montana

"THIS MAN IS IMPOSSIBLE." Sylvia Summers, the nursing supervisor at Mountain Home Health Care, complained as she stood putting together a copy of a patient's chart for Laura. "Even over the phone he comes across as brooding, wants everything his own way, including the exact timing of our visits. Can you imagine how hard it is to time our trips up to the Yakk River and then along that Sixteen Mile...*cowpath* to the exact hour? Why he chooses to live out there—"

"Even with all that money," one of the field nurses interrupted as she scooted past Laura's desk, "he lives an austere existence on the side of the mountain. Doesn't even have a TV."

"The man's a hermit, who hardly speaks except to snap my nurses' heads off," Sylvia continued. "And he's already run off two other physical therapists. Now it's your turn.'' She handed Laura the chart.

Another nurse peeked around the supply shelves and chimed in. "That chart should be labeled P.I.A., because if ever there was one, that guy's a genuine pain in the—"

"I've handled P.I.A.'s before," Laura answered quietly as she walked to her desk. *And I'm an expert on rich, demanding men,* she added to herself as she thought of Stuart Crestwood for the first time in ages. "Difficult patients don't bother me. Remember Mr. Buchanan? Wouldn't even get out of bed at first." She sat down and pushed her glasses up on her nose, trying to focus her mind on the chart, in spite of the nurses' discouraging verbal barrage.

"Ho! Ho! Ho! Hon-*nee* child!" another nurse hooted. "Mr. Scott makes old man Buchanan seem like a sweet cuddly teddy bear."

The others muttered their agreement.

Sylvia raised a palm. "Okay, girls. We've scared her enough." She crossed to Laura's desk.

"Listen, Laura, this is a tough case. No one wants to deal with this man, much less stay up on that mountain and do the hours of therapy necessary to—"

"You told me all that," she put in, "and about

the car accident.'' She flipped back a page in the chart. ''It says here he's a widower. Was his wife killed in the accident?''

''Yes.'' Sylvia sighed and ran a hand through her short-cropped frosted hair. ''A terrible accident. Anyway, you'll be taking this on as a private contract, with no supervisory visits. In other words you're totally on your own. And once you and Mr. Scott sign that contract, I hope you'll stay to finish the therapy regimen.''

Laura flipped more pages. Fractured scapula and humerus. Severe rotator-cuff tear, avulsed muscles, some nerve damage, adhesive capsulitis.... ''This man's surgery was almost a year ago. Why are we just now doing joint mobilization?''

''He shut himself off from people when he left the hospital. But now, all of a sudden, he wants full use of his shoulder back. It wasn't happening fast enough to suit him with only two visits a week.''

Laura nodded and closed the chart. ''I'm going to do joint mobilization once every day, assisted exercises twice a day, ice packs after each treatment.''

''Sounds good.'' Sylvia glanced at her watch. ''You'd better get going. As I said, Adam Scott demands punctuality.'' Frowning, Sylvia bent her head, and said confidentially, "You know, you're a brave girl to accept this assignment."

Bravery has nothing to do with it, Laura thought as she lugged the heavy portable massage table and arm bike out to her old Toyota. The obscene amount of money this patient was willing to pay for a private full-time physical therapist for six weeks was her sole motivation.

When Laura had first taken off with Stuart's money, she hadn't realized how much she would change. Over the past four years, as she'd finished her education and forced herself to mature and grow, she'd come to realize that she wouldn't really be free until she paid Stuart back every cent. The salary Adam Scott was offering would go a long way toward getting rid of her debt.

But the nurses' descriptions of her new patient kept ringing through her mind as she steered her little car along the narrow gravel road that skirted the sheer wall of rock high above Sixteen Mile Creek.

When at last the road ended, she felt as if she'd traveled back in time. A weathered log cabin squatted in an open glade like an old hen brooding on a nest. Two quaint dormer windows twinkled in the September sunshine, and a sturdy native-rock chimney buttressed one side of the steep blue roof. A deep porch across the entire front seemed like the perfect spot for enjoying mountain vistas, but it didn't have a stick of furniture on it.

And there, on that porch, stood Adam Scott, waiting for her.

His face was hidden in the shadows, but his long muscular legs, clad in worn jeans and hiking boots, were crossed causally at the ankle. He leaned one shoulder—not the bad one, she noticed—against the rough-hewn door frame.

His body looked so…young. So strong!

The relaxed powerful figure leaning against that door certainly didn't fit the picture of the lame bitter recluse her colleagues had conjured up.

She peered through her windshield. He didn't look a day over thirty-five. Well, he was close enough at thirty-eight, but somehow she hadn't expected him to be such a…hunk.

Laura fumbled on the floor for her satchel and tried to swallow the lump that had suddenly formed in her throat.

She glanced back up at him. He wasn't leaning against the door frame anymore, and now his stance and folded arms radiated impatience.

She opened the car door and drew a deep breath. She climbed out, then carefully closed the door and walked up the path with what she hoped was self-assurance.

He came forward, scowling from under thick dark eyebrows, and the lump in her throat doubled in size, because now that he was in the sun, she could see that not only was he young and fit, he was extremely handsome.

He looked like a younger version of—who was that actor who'd played Marshall Matt Dillon in *Gunsmoke?*—James Arness. This guy had the same strong jaw. The same big hands. All of which kept him from seeming too perfect, too pretty.

His thick dark hair looked wild and untrimmed, with a few silvery strands sprigging at the temples.

His whole presence seemed unreal. As if he'd been plunked into this rustic setting by some visionary movie director: *All right now. Stand there with the sun in your eyes—no, don't shade them. Look mean. As if she's a bug you intend to squash with your boot. That's good. Oh—nice touch! Raising your arm and propping your palm rigidly against the porch post, like you aren't even going to let her inside the cabin. Does somebody in wardrobe have a really worn-looking denim shirt?*

The man fixed his dark eyes on her. When they

caught the sun they flashed silver, like a...a wolf's or something.

Laura averted her own gaze, feeling a little breathless. Not because she was climbing a steep grade, but because that look in his eyes had been so intense that it had left her feeling stunned.

As she climbed the porch steps, it occurred to her that the man before her might not even be her patient. He could be the hired help or a relative, perhaps.

But when he said, "Are *you* my new physical therapist?" in a low baritone, that small hope burst like a punctured balloon.

"Yes. I'm Laura Duncan—" Laura smiled and put out her hand as she took the last stair "—from Mountain Home Health Care."

"And who is that?" He nodded toward the Toyota.

Laura dropped her hand and swiveled her head. Ned! She was so used to her ever present "safety man" riding in the passenger seat that she'd forgotten he was supposed to look real from a distance.

"That's a safety dummy." She looked up at her patient and smiled. "You know, to make it look like I have a passenger—I drive on a lot of isolated roads." She stuck out her hand again. "It's nice to meet you."

He stared at her hand, then gave her a critical frown. "My right arm is injured, remember?" With that he turned his back and disappeared into the cabin.

Laura's eyes went wide and she dropped her hand. Her throat got tighter as she felt herself blushing at her mistake.

She hesitated at the doorway, then peered in, wondering if he meant for her to follow. She couldn't see him; her eyes were still adjusting from the bright mountain sunshine to the gloomy interior of the cabin.

"Well, come in, dammit." His rich baritone came from somewhere in the darkness. "Don't just stand there."

Laura's back stiffened, and she stood firmly rooted in the doorway. No amount of money was worth being cursed at. She'd had enough of that kind of treatment from Stuart.

She heard heavy footsteps, and in the next instant his face materialized in the shaft of sunlight pouring through the cabin door. She quailed at his fierce expression, but she stood her ground.

"What?" he said.

"Let's get something straight, Mr. Scott. I heard about the way you treat the nurses. I'd appreciate it if you'd watch your language and your temper."

He gave her another dark squint. ''For the exorbitant amount I'm paying you, I can say and do just about anything I please.''

''Not to me.'' Laura turned on her heel, stomped across the porch and clattered down the steps, marching to her car as fast as possible.

''Wait!'' he hollered as he sprinted down the steps behind her.

''Okay, okay,'' he said, coming up short beside her car as she tossed in her satchel and climbed behind the wheel. She saw him throw up his hands as she slammed the door.

He bent down beside the closed window as she started the engine. ''Okay! No cursing!'' he yelled through the glass.

Laura lowered the window a couple of inches but didn't kill the engine.

''Look, Ms.— What'd you say your name was?''

''Duncan. Laura Duncan.'' After four years she'd grown comfortable with her maiden name again.

''Ms. Duncan. Stay.'' He backed up from the window, jammed his left hand into the pocket of his jeans and shrugged uncomfortably. ''Please.''

Stuart used to shrug like that. An innocent-looking gesture that in Laura's mind was as phony as a three-dollar bill.

"Please," he repeated. "I've got to get this shoulder working again. And I can't do it without a therapist."

Laura held her foot on the brake while she stared out the windshield and considered.

He needed her skills, and she needed his money.

Four years of physical-therapy training had depleted every cent she'd filched from Stuart. All she had now was a simple little frame house back in Kalispell, this eight-year-old Toyota and her self-respect.

She gave Adam Scott a sidelong glance. "I suppose you know I'm the only physical therapist who's prepared to work with you."

He didn't flinch, didn't look angry, didn't even laugh derisively. He merely gave her another squinting assessment, then blinked as if coming out a dream.

"That doesn't surprise me at all, Ms. Duncan," he said. "I can't say that I blame them. I can be difficult. But I promise, if you stay, I'll treat you professionally. Now, won't you please come inside?"

CHAPTER TWO

As she stepped into the cabin, Laura's misgivings about taking on this case only increased.

Thick-hewn beams, darkened with age, spanned the low ceiling, making the long rectangular room feel oppressive and gloomy. Her first impulse was to dart around to the windows set squarely into three of the walls and throw back the heavy wooden shutters.

Instead, she set her satchel at her feet and let her eyes adjust to the dim light while she waited for her patient to come back in.

He'd gone through a door toward the back to get another chair, she supposed. The fact that there was only a table and one lone chair in this barren room was spooky, not to mention the darkness and the general lack of…life about this place.

Laura rubbed her hands up and down her sweatshirt-covered arms. Even though it was early September and the last scraps of snow on the high peaks were long gone, the mountain air had a definite chill. She hoped she could complete Mr. Scott's treatment program according to her six-week plan. Sixteen Mile Creek road would be impassable once the first heavy snows fell.

She eyed the massive stone fireplace. It was swept clean and cold-looking, like the mouth of a cave.

The walls of the room, rough knotty-pine planks, had absolutely no decoration, the wooden floor, no rugs. The place looked the same as Laura guessed it had for—what?—the past century or so.

On the round oak table was a solitary paper plate holding the remains of a plain bologna sandwich. What kind of man chose to live such an existence?

She turned and looked back out the front door, which stood open. Should she close it? No. If she did, this room would be as dark as night.

Beyond the shadows of the porch she spotted the corner of a well-tended garden, which she hadn't noticed when she'd driven up. That was odd. She craned her neck to see more. It sloped down the sunny side of the mountain in neat rows. What did he do with all those vegetables? she wondered. As she watched, a big shaggy yellow dog sauntered into the picture and flopped down in a shady spot at the edge of the garden. Well, if the man had a dog, maybe he wasn't all bad.

"Ms. Duncan?"

She whirled around, instantly blushing, embarrassed that she'd allowed his deep voice to startle her.

He clumped into the room, frowning and carrying a chair with his good arm. He banged it down opposite the one at the table. "Have a seat."

Laura crossed the bare floor and after she adjusted the chair—the wooden legs made a terrible scraping noise—she sat, none too comfortably.

He lowered himself into the chair opposite and pushed the sandwich aside.

"Did I interrupt your lunch?" she asked. Her own had been a quick carton of yogurt and some crackers and fruit from the basket of goodies she'd packed.

"Let's see the contract."

Laura's cheeks grew hotter. Okay. So he was going to be consistently rude. She supposed she could deal with that.

"Can we have some light?" she asked pleasantly.

Without a word he got up—the chair legs

made that terrible scraping noise again—and rounded the table to the nearest window. He slammed the heavy wooden shutters aside. Light poured through wavy-paned glass onto the table-top, making the white paper plate glow.

While he returned to his seat, Laura dug the contract out of her bag. When she held it out, he snatched the pages from her hand. He reached across and rubbed his right shoulder, frowning as he read the document.

Finally he tossed the papers onto the table. "I asked for a *male* therapist you know," he said flatly, and crossed his well-muscled arms over his chest.

"I know," Laura answered quietly, "but as I told you, I'm the only one who would come. Didn't Mrs. Summers explain that to you?"

Adam Scott scowled. "You are absolutely not what I had in mind."

"I'm sorry about that, but let me assure you I am very good at what I do." She smiled. "And you did ask me to stay. Tell you what, I'll give you a complimentary treatment—" she picked up the contract, "—and if you don't like it, I'll leave."

He glared at her and snatched the papers from her hand again, then slapped them on the table in front of him and held out his hand for a pen. "Where do I sign?"

She pointed out the three places where he would consent to her treatment plan, assure her of full payment and allow her to release his medical records to any insurance carrier. "Sign here, here and here."

As the pen scratched across the paper while he signed his name, Laura noticed he still wore his wedding band.

He stopped after signing only two of the lines. "I don't use insurance," he stated in a tone that invited no discussion. Laura pointed at the fee figures. "Fine. Initial these, please."

He gave her a grudging nod and did so.

One more piece of business. "Where will I be staying?" she asked as she handed him the carbon copy and put the signed original back in her satchel. She could always go back into the tiny town of Libby and stay at the modest motel there, but that would mean arduous daily trips up that Sixteen Mile Creek Road, and it would cost them valuable therapy time.

She'd noticed a smaller stone house a little farther up the mountain. It actually looked pleasant, inviting. Maybe she could stay there. One thing was certain: he was just about the most attractive man she'd ever seen, and she wasn't about to stay under the same roof with him.

At last he smiled. A relaxed slightly crooked smile that bared strong white teeth.

"I was planning to put an extra bed up here." He didn't wait for her response to that. He crossed his arms over his broad chest and said, "Now you can see why I asked for a male therapist."

"What about that small house farther up on the mountain? Could I possibly stay there?"

His face darkened.

Instead of answering her, he stood and crossed the room to the door. He braced his good arm on the frame and stared out at the lovely garden.

After what seemed an eternity, he said, "No. The stone house is closed." He hung his head as if thinking, then spoke quietly. "I guess you could take the bedroom upstairs and I could... I could open up the stone house."

"I'm sorry Mr. Scott, but my staying upstairs doesn't address the problem. I'm not comfortable staying alone on this mountain with you in this isolated cabin—"

His long weary sigh interrupted her. For another moment he kept his head lowered. Then Laura saw his shoulders move, thought she actually heard a chuckle.

"Ms. Duncan, you certainly drive a hard bargain. All right. I know a reliable older couple down the creek. They're—" his voice became gentle, "—they're very nice people, very stable. If I ask them, they'll come and stay in the house with you—they can sleep downstairs." He said all this with his back toward her. "Over there." He gestured at an empty alcove at the other side of the room. "The old guy has bad knees, so the stairs would be too much for him."

When Laura remained patiently silent, he turned and looked at her. His dark eyes had a thoughtful squint, as if he was making a difficult decision. He swallowed. "And I'll sleep in the stone house. Would that be satisfactory?"

"I suppose," Laura said quietly.

He nodded and regarded her with cool detachment. "Good. Now if you don't mind, I'd like my first treatment right away. My shoulder is killing me."

CHAPTER THREE

WHILE LAURA DUNCAN was applying her strong skilled hands to his bare back, Adam had to make an effort not to feel what he was feeling, not to think what he was thinking.

It scared him, the effect this woman had had on him when he'd first seen her. The more he thought about it, the more he realized that it hadn't just been that she was attractive. She'd looked…special.

No woman had looked that way to him since Elizabeth.

Of course, the few women he'd seen since he'd decided to go into hiding up on Sixteen Mile Creek couldn't be considered much of a sampling. The husky postwoman delivering a package, those matronly Mountain Home nurses, the elderly Katherine. Nice ladies. None of them a threat to his precious memories.

Laura's hands kept bringing his attention back to her. He could hear her gentle breathing becoming more labored as she worked diligently.

She'd made him sit in one of the straight-backed chairs, facing backward, and was rhythmically digging her thumb into a muscle that had felt like a burning knot only seconds ago.

"You have a trigger point here, where a tight muscle is crossing a nerve and compressing it. I'll be sure to use moist heat packs on it before the next treatment."

Yes, even from a distance this woman had looked singular, unique. Despite her faded jeans and that neon-orange sweatshirt with that dumb slogan—PHYSICAL THERAPISTS HAVE PATIENTS—she exuded a kind of elegance.

He had watched her unload her belongings from the hatchback of that faded red Toyota like a magician pulling stuff out of a hat. First had come her personal bags, surprisingly compact, then she'd heaved out a big rectangle that looked like a folding table. After that she'd struggled with a contraption that looked like the front half of a small bike, mounted on a stand.

Then a CD player, a pillow, a gym bag that seemed too heavy for a woman of her petite stature, and a large gift basket—what was that for?

Finally, she'd taken out the life-size doll she'd called a safety dummy. The thing was done up to resemble a sort of Raggedy Andy cowboy with a painted-on face, plaid shirt, battered black hat, even an old pair of boots at the end of stuffed denim legs.

"The passenger door leaks when it rains, so better to keep him inside," she'd explained as she lugged the dummy up the porch steps. "Meet Ned." She stopped in the doorway and flopped the white muslin "hand" at him.

Adam had given the thing a dubious frown, but he'd admired the way she'd managed to cheerfully haul it and everything else up the cabin steps and inside without emitting so much as a groan.

"I'll set up the massage table tomorrow. We can manage without it today," she'd explained.

Now she was flattening her warm palm against the injured area, applying a gentle rotating pressure that seemed to pull the pain out. After a moment his eyes involuntarily closed with pure relief.

"Mr. Scott?"

His eyes flew open and looked straight into hers, only inches from his own. They were clear blue eyes, tilted up at the corners. No makeup.

"I'm afraid that was the pleasant part of the treatment." She spoke softly, apologetically. Her voice was melodic and low, with a hint of a Southern drawl.

Her lips—moist-looking pink lips—parted, as

if she was unsure about something. "Umm...for the next step, which may cause some discomfort, I'll need you to be stretched out on your abdomen."

She stood straight, swiveling at the waist as she scanned the room. Her breasts—perfect, very rounded—stretched the fabric of the sweatshirt.

"Where's your bed?" she said.

Her gentle hands resumed massaging his shoulder muscles rhythmically while she waited for his answer.

Adam was so completely relaxed from what her hands were doing to him that he didn't answer right away.

She leaned forward. "Mr. Scott? The bed?" she repeated.

He took a deep breath and reluctantly shoved himself to his feet. "Upstairs."

He fumbled with his shirt, couldn't find the armholes, gave up. "The, uh, stairs—" he pointed "—are in the kitchen."

She followed as he led her through the door to the left of the fireplace, down a short dim hallway and into a bright kitchen at the back of the cabin.

NOW THIS ROOM is more like it, Laura thought.

Above the deep white enamel sink a solid bank

of pleasingly spaced casement windows looked out on the verdant mountainside as it rose at an acute angle behind the cabin.

The varnished knotty-pine cabinets formed a cozy U around a waist-high chopping block. *Thank God I'll have plenty of ice,* she thought when she noticed a large refrigerator, albeit an ancient rounded model, humming in the corner. An old wood-burning cast-iron cook stove completed the charming picture.

There were bird feeders outside the windows and fresh herbs growing on the sills in hand-thrown clay pots. A squat old teakettle stood on the stove, and a colorful quilt draped an antique rocker.

Adam jerked a leather strap on a plank door that groaned opened onto a narrow wooden staircase rising between two whitewashed walls. The stairs creaked as he clumped up them, Laura following.

At the top was an attic room that seemed even gloomier than the one below it. Laura's first question when her eyes took in the enclosure with its bare-studded walls was going to be: Where is the bathroom?

She hadn't noticed one downstairs. But when she glanced out the large floor-to-ceiling window set into the gable end by the stair landing, she saw her answer.

Below, at the end of a narrow footpath worn through the thick mountain grasses, looking like something from a picture postcard, sat a weathered gray structure. Complete with tin roof and quarter-moon hole in the door. An outhouse. Lovely.

She turned to her new patient and smiled bravely. ''Please lie facedown on the bed with your shoulder near the edge. No pillow.''

He went to the heavy four-poster bed tucked up under the roof between two dormer windows, pulled off his boots, struggling with the left one, then did as she asked. Laura stood over him, warming some lotion between her palms and wondering how in the world she could continue. Though she'd admitted to herself right away that he was handsome, actually touching him had been a shock.

His skin was tanned, smooth and warm. As soon as she laid her hands on his firm back, she felt an electric thrill run through her fingertips, unlike anything she'd ever felt before. Certainly a sensation unlike any she'd felt while touching any other patient.

She'd made it through the warm-up phase of the therapy on sheer professional concentration, but now she wondered if she could complete the painful stretches and manipulations necessary to remove scar tissue without communicating her nervousness to him.

He was lying very still, his back muscles relaxed and his breathing regular. Careful not to drip the lotion on his bare back, she leaned forward and realized the man had fallen asleep.

WHEN HE WOKE UP, he realized he was upstairs in his bed, but couldn't figure out how he'd gotten there or what time it was. The sunlight slanting through the western dormers was low and golden, so it must be evening.

He was startled when he saw a cowboy slumping between the wall and the bed, denim legs sprawled straight out as if the man was drunk. Then he remembered.

The safety dummy. *Her*.

He'd been so relaxed when she'd finished the first part of the treatment that he'd trudged up the stairs in a fog, flopped on the bed the way she told him to and then?

He sat up, rubbed his eyes, flexed his injured arm and shoulder. It felt pretty good. And *he* felt fantastic. He hadn't slept like this since... He heard voices downstairs. Doc and Katherine. The delicious spicy aroma of Katherine's lentil soup drifted up. Was it dinnertime already?

Laughter.

Laura Duncan's laughter.

Man. Having her here was going to be tough. Why did they have to send him a *beautiful* female physical therapist? It was hard enough looking at her, but when she touched him...

He couldn't afford to let himself have these feelings. He needed a fully functioning arm and shoulder if he was going to do what he had to do, and he didn't need to be distracted by the charms of his therapist. This arrangement would never work. Somehow he'd find another way to get his therapy done.

He pulled on his boots, which set off a twinge of pain in his shoulder, found his shirt, sneered at Ned while he buttoned it, then headed down the stairs.

The laughter fell off when he ducked his head around the narrow door at the foot of the stairs.

"Adam," Katherine said kindly, and stepped away from the stove toward him. "Did you sleep well?"

"We were just getting acquainted with Laura." Doc smiled up at him from the rocker.

Laura Duncan was standing at the chopping block, where the big gift basket sat with the cellophane all askew as if they'd been digging around in it. Evidently she'd been slicing chunks of cantaloupe into a crockery bowl, but now she stopped. She, too, was smiling. Everybody looked happy. He was glad to see Doc and Katherine enjoying themselves, but he had no intention of joining the party. For him there was no such feeling as happy. Only one thing drove his days and nights now. One thing. And Doc and Katherine knew that.

"Ms. Duncan, I need to speak to you. Alone." He marched past her into the main room and waited with his boot propped on the big stone hearth.

IN THE KITCHEN, Laura looked from Doc to Katherine, confusion and embarrassment rendering her speechless. Things had been going so well!

She'd immediately liked Doc and Katherine Jones, lean white-haired retirees who wore Birkenstocks and sincere smiles. As soon as they'd walked in the back door of the cabin, their arms loaded with groceries, Laura had sensed their good humor, their kindness, their wisdom.

As the older couple bustled about putting away the food and chattering, it was obvious they felt at home and knew where everything was stored in the small kitchen. In no time they were all sipping steaming mugs of the herbal tea Laura had taken from her basket.

"We come up the mountain all the time," Katherine explained. "We try to help Adam. I cook. Doc tends garden and does odd jobs." She sighed. "Poor Adam—such a long recovery."

After they'd helped Laura situate her gear, they'd given her a tour of the place—forty acres in the middle of a national forest. The last of such private land, Doc explained. The log cabin was built late in the nineteenth century, Katherine told her. The stone house, she said, was added later.

The whole time Adam Scott had slept soundly, and as the sun lowered, there had been an almost palpable peace about the breathtakingly beautiful old homestead.

Then, Laura thought, the minute the man stomped down the stairs, there was tension again.

Doc cleared his throat and scratched the top of his balding pate. "You'd better go see what he wants, Laura."

"Yes," Katherine added. "The soup will keep." She turned to the stove and stirred it.

"Excuse me, then." Laura laid aside the knife, wiped her hands on the apron Katherine had supplied and went into the main room.

She wished he'd lit a lamp. The pale evening

light that filtered in through the lone unshuttered window didn't allow her to see him, much less read his expression.

His voice rumbled, disembodied, from beside the fireplace. "We need to discuss this arrangement," he said.

Laura dropped her hands to her sides and squared her shoulders. "Mr. Scott, I've been thinking. Maybe I'm not the right therapist for you, after all. I'll arrange some sort of replacement immediately and, of course, I won't hold you to that contract."

"What?" Even in the darkness, Laura sensed his sudden dismay.

She wished she had a plausible excuse. She'd tried to think of one all afternoon while he slept. But what could she say? *I think I'm attracted to you, so it wouldn't be a good idea for me to do your therapy?* Though it was true, that sounded so unprofessional it made Laura cringe. "I'm leaving, but I'll stay till I find a replacement."

Wait a minute, Adam thought as he studied Laura in the dim light, *she's leaving?* The strangest mix of emotions assailed him. He was a scientist, a logical man, but he couldn't explain these feelings. Upstairs he'd been certain she should go, but the second she announced that she was leaving, his heart had started to beat faster and his breath had actually become short. She reached up self-consciously to adjust her tiny earring, making it glint, and he was struck again by how feminine she was, how even her slightest movement affected him.

"Ms. Duncan—" he found his voice "—I know I've been…less than cordial. But now that you'll have the Joneses here with you…" His voice trailed off. He felt genuinely at a loss. When had his goal become keeping her here?

"Please, believe me, Mr. Scott, it's not anything you've done," Laura was saying. "And I like Doc and Katherine a lot. I just…I just don't think I've got what it takes to complete your therapy. I know my limits."

"But my arm and my shoulder—when I woke up they already felt better." He stepped forward, feeling like a panic-stricken little boy. "I'll double your salary."

"Mr. Scott! I couldn't let you do that." Even in the darkening room, he could see her eyes widen with shock. "That would make my fee almost twenty-five thousand dollars!"

"I want you to stay," he stated simply. She didn't reply.

DINNER WAS QUIET, uneasy.

Katherine had lit a kerosene lamp in the middle of the table, which alleviated the gloom, and the food was delicious, especially Katherine's homemade bread, but Laura sensed Adam's tension. And the way Doc and Katherine addressed him—so kindly, so carefully, as if he was fragile and needed encouragement—bothered her. It also began to bother her that the Joneses had so easily given up their own beds for this man. What was their relationship? It seemed more than neighborly.

"Adam, aren't you having any brown Betty? I made it just for you," Katherine said.

"You don't have to cook especially for me, Katherine. I told you that."

After dinner Adam and Doc busied themselves setting up a bed for the Joneses in the small alcove on the other side of the fireplace. Laura didn't ask where the bed had come from. This place was full of unanswered questions, some less important than others.

After she helped Katherine with the dishes, Laura washed up at the kitchen sink, visited the outhouse with a flashlight, then retreated to the attic.

It was Katherine, she assumed, who'd thoughtfully placed a vase of wildflowers on the chest and made up the bed with fresh sheets—*his* bed.

Laura shook the thought off. She had to remain professional and detached.

She turned on the small bedside lamp and settled herself in, ready to pore over the thick sheaf of Adam Scott's chart again.

"All right, Ned-o." She glanced at the dummy propped against the wall. "Let's see what this guy is all about."

Adam Scott had had a long recovery indeed. Ruptured spleen. Pins in his broken shoulder. Months of surgeries, antibiotics, treatments. Yet he appeared to be in good physical condition, considering all his trauma.

Strengthening the arm and shoulder muscles and restoring complete range of motion would be the last painful step. Except... She thumbed through the chart, looking for psychotherapy referrals. None.

"Patient refuses" notations next to entries documenting offers of counseling and pastoral care made it clear that everyone who'd tried to help Adam Scott had been rebuffed. There was something disturbing about this case, about this man, something she couldn't see just by reading his charts.

She flipped back to the biographical data. All the blanks were neatly filled in, and she'd read it all this morning. She sighed. "All the same, I reckon we got us a real pitiful one, Ned."

She closed the chart, scooted under the thick down comforter and tossed her way into a restless sleep.

SOMEWHERE IN THE NIGHT a sound, something softer than a moth's wing, awakened her.

She opened her eyes a crack and without raising her head looked around the unfamiliar room. Rain pattered softly on the metal attic roof and the mountain air had grown so chilly that her nose felt cold.

Lightning flashed, and standing there, clearly silhouetted in the floor-to-ceiling window at the far end of the attic, was a man.

For an instant Laura was paralyzed by fear, as thunder rolled over the roof. Her heart raced.

Another bolt of lightning illuminated the figure. Though she couldn't see clearly without her glasses, she recognized the build. Adam Scott. Of course. But what on earth…?

Waves of sheet lightning in the distance kept him constantly in view now. His pose was alert, still.

He faced the window, holding a pair of binoculars. They were bigger than normal, Laura thought, with a long extra piece in the middle, perhaps the night-vision kind she'd seen in thrillers.

She was about to let him know she was awake when, as the room darkened, she thought she saw him turn his head in her direction.

Laura lay stiffly in the dark, feeling that he was staring at her. The bed was under the eaves, cloaked in complete darkness, but even so, she wondered if he could feel her staring back.

She feigned sleep, waiting to see what he would do. After a long moment she heard him cross to the stairwell, cautiously, soundlessly. Just as he reached it, faint flashes of lightning in the distance made his silhouette visible. She watched him descend until finally his head disappeared below the landing.

Lightning continued to pulse in the distance, and she heard the sound of one stealthy creak as he opened the door at the bottom of the stairs.

The whole thing gave Laura a roaring case of the creeps.

THE NEXT MORNING she awoke before the sun peeked over the mountain. She padded barefoot across the cold wooden floor to gaze out the window onto the dewy green expanse of meadow between the cabin and the outhouse. What had he been looking at last night?

Doc was hiking stiffly up the misty path. When he spotted Laura standing in the window, he raised his arm and gave her a jaunty salute.

Everything below looked normal. So idyllic and beautiful, in fact, that she could hardly believe the unsettling incident last night had happened.

Beyond the meadow, Sixteen Mile Creek sparkled in the deep valley, the narrow road beside it winding lazily down, finally intersecting with a bigger road. The view from this window clearly showed the route up to Adam Scott's property—the only route. He must have been checking that. But why?

Shivering slightly, she slipped into her plaid robe and slippers and made her way gingerly down the creaky stairs, concerned that she might awaken Katherine.

But Katherine was already bustling around the kitchen.

The fire crackling in the old stove, the eggs gently boiling in a pan, the teakettle steaming, all made the small room feel toasty warm and inviting. Laura hated to venture out into the chilly morning, but she needed to make a trip to the outhouse. After she returned, she started to wash her hands at the sink.

"Oh, use the basin, dear." Katherine suggested. "That pipe water is freezing." Katherine poured hot water from the kettle and cooler water from an old-fashioned pitcher into a matching basin. Laura submerged her hands in the warm water, then washed her face with the glycerin soap Katherine had provided, marveling at how this primitive setting seemed to enhance the simple pleasures.

When she was finished washing, she accepted a warm bran muffin and a fragrant mug of tea from Katherine.

"There's a small jar of strawberry preserve in my basket," Laura offered.

"No!" Katherine exclaimed. "You don't need to use the things from your basket."

"But I want to."

"Well, I make gallons of cherry jelly every year." Katherine reached into the refrigerator and pulled out a pint mason jar and unscrewed the lid. Then she opened a drawer and produced an ornate silver condiment spoon. All the homey touches in the kitchen were likely this older woman's doing.

"Thank you." Laura took the jelly, thinking how much nicer her stay would be with this lovely woman around.

"No trouble." Katherine smiled. "By the way, Doc and I are strict vegetarians. So, if you don't mind, I'll do the cooking while we're here.''

Laura took a bite of the muffin—heavenly. ''Mind?'' she said, and swallowed. ''I'm a vegetarian, too!''

Katherine' s smile grew wider. ''Why don't you sit down on that stool?'' She pointed at a well-worn bar stool that looked hand-hewn. ''We can chat while I finish filling these hummingbird feeders.''

While Katherine measured a batch of red nectar into a large bowl and slowly stirred the mixture, the two women talked about ordinary things.

How well Laura had slept: ''Pretty well,'' she hedged. ''It's so very quiet up here.''

Where she came from originally: ''Texas—Dallas. But I could never go back. So hot. So hectic.''

Where Doc and Katherine came from: ''Seattle. Doc isn't a medical doctor, you know. He's a botanist.''

How the older couple had long dreamed of retiring up on Sixteen Mile Creek: ''Because there is no more beautiful place on earth.''

Laura had to agree. ''Where's your house?''

''Oh, quite a distance back down the road. It takes a good thirty minutes to get there, but one can go faster in a canoe when the creek's high. There's also the shortcut—nothing more than a rough logging road. I don't recommend it to the uninitiated.''

When Katherine showed no signs of volunteering any information about Adam Scott, Laura decided to ask.

"How long have you known Mr. Scott?"

"Oh, many years." Katherine smiled as she used a little funnel to fill the feeder.

This seemed to Laura a cryptic answer. She tried again.

"What, exactly, does he do for a living?"

"Oh, he doesn't like to talk about that much." Katherine screwed the lid on the feeder, carefully turned it over and held it up by its chain, examining her handiwork. "All done," she said cheerfully.

"And Mrs. Scott? Did you know her?"

Katherine dropped the hummingbird feeder onto its side, and as the sticky cherry-colored liquid gurgled out, the woman did nothing to stop it. She touched her gnarled fingers to her heart and paled, staring at Laura while the mess ran over the side of the cabinet top and onto the floorboards.

"Oh, dear," Laura said as she jumped off her

stool and righted the feeder. "Let me help you clean that up."

Katherine swung her gaze to the red liquid dripping at her feet, but still she didn't move.

"Did I say something wrong?" Laura asked gently as she snapped off a handful of paper towels and started soaking up the puddle.

"No." At last Katherine seemed to come to herself. "No, dear. You didn't." She turned toward the sink and ran water over a dishrag. She twisted the rag, wrung out the water, then started furiously mopping up the mess on the countertop. "It's...well, Adam's wife is..." Katherine stopped cleaning and looked at Laura with eyes full of something unspoken. She seemed to be gauging how much to reveal. "Adam's wife is deceased."

"I know that. I read it in his chart. I was just wondering about her."

"I see." Katherine resumed scrubbing the counter, and Laura could see that her hands trembled.

"She died in the car wreck?" Laura asked gently.

Katherine nodded. "Instantly. The car plunged off the side of a mountain back in Washington." She kept on scrubbing.

"Oh, that's terrible," Laura whispered. "No one told me exactly how it happened."

Katherine continued to clean.

Laura sensed the woman was holding something back. She squatted down with the paper towels and started wiping up the mess on the rough wood as best she could.

"I'm sorry." She looked up at Katherine's back. "I didn't mean to upset you."

Tension built in the quiet kitchen while the ashes in the old cast-iron stove collapsed with a pop and a hiss and bird song filtered in from outside.

Finally Katherine turned and looked down at Laura. Her wrinkled old eyes communicated an unspeakable sadness when she spoke. "I...I did know Elizabeth. Quite well. And I knew their little girl, too. Anna. She died in the accident, also...with her mother."

CHAPTER FOUR

HIS CHILD HAD DIED, too?

Laura stared up at Katherine's seasoned face in disbelief.

"I'm sorry," she managed. "How old was his daughter?"

Katherine's hand stilled on the dishrag and she stared out the window. "Three." She spoke as if in a trance.

"How awful," Laura said.

Katherine nodded. "Elizabeth and Adam had waited several years to have her. Elizabeth was a research scientist and did not want her demanding career goals to interfere with a child's happiness. She had waited until...she and Adam had reached a certain level of success and then...then they had Anna."

"I see," Laura said quietly. She still didn't know what to say.

Katherine turned on the spigot in the sink. Water blasted out and she rinsed the cloth under it, shaking her head. "This water drains by gravity from the spring. Never reliable. Sometimes a torrent, sometimes a dribble. And always freezing.''

"Katherine, are you okay?" Laura asked.

Katherine nodded. Laura reached out and clasped the older woman in a hug.

And that was how Adam Scott found them, embracing.

"Ms. Duncan!" he boomed from behind the screen door, then jerked it open.

Laura and Katherine broke apart as he stepped into the room, but not before they gave each other one last parting pat. When their gazes met as they released each other, Laura thought she read warning in Katherine's.

"Are you ready to go to work?" Adam frowned at Laura's attire. "I'd like my morning treatment as early as possible."

"Uh, no. I'm sorry. I'm not ready." Laura cinched her robe. "I, uh, I need to go up and put my scrubs on, and—" she pulled her mop of hair back "—I'll be right down." She turned, jerked on the leather strap on the narrow door and dashed up the stairs.

In her embarrassment and haste she hadn't closed the door completely and when she got to the landing at the top she froze when she heard Adam say her name.

"What were you and Ms. Duncan talking about?"

"I think you know." Katherine's voice sounded tearful.

Laura clutched the railing.

She heard Adam's sympathetic reply—"Ahh, Katherine,"—and then his heavy bootfalls as he crossed the room. "Are you all right?" he asked tenderly.

She heard Katherine sniffling and saying something in a small pained voice. Then Adam murmuring softly. He finished with something that sounded like, "You mustn't keep upsetting yourself."

Laura crossed the room to start dressing and tried to ignore the conversation below her, but the voices continued to drift clearly up the stairs.

"Adam, I think we should be honest with this young woman." Katherine's voice was louder, firmer now.

Adam's tone sounded exasperated. "No. That's not a good idea."

Laura coughed loudly, hoping they'd realize she could hear them. Evidently they must have gotten the idea, because she heard Adam's footsteps again and then a creak as the stairway door closed.

ADAM HAD PUT his finger to his lips as soon as he'd heard Laura cough. Katherine was a little hard of hearing, and it was easy for her to forget how well sound carried in the quiet cabin, but he had no excuse for being so careless. After he closed the door to the stairs, he led Katherine into the front room to continue their conversation.

"Laura and the people at Mountain Home Health Care don't need to know any details. The fewer people who know, the better. That way nobody can inadvertently lead Gradoff to me before I'm ready."

"Adam, I told you before—this is a dangerous scheme. You don't know—"

"I know what I'm doing, and I'm sticking to my plan."

"But now Laura will be staying up on the mountain with us. How can we possibly keep the truth from her?"

"How much did you tell her?" Adam struggled to keep his voice from sounding alarmed.

"I told her about…both of them. It states on your chart that you're a widower and I just blurted out the part about Anna." Katherine's eyes filled with tears when she said the name.

"Katherine." Adam looked down at her snow-white head and his heart contracted. It was bad enough that his brainstorm—his *greed*—had killed Elizabeth and Anna. He would have to live with that for the rest of his life. His guilt was his punishment to bear. But to see how Doc and Katherine also suffered...

He stepped closer to her. "It's all right."

"No, it's not, but I won't speak to her about it again. She's such a nice person, but still, I know I shouldn't have said anything." A note of fear rose in Katherine's voice. "What if she goes back down to town and talks to someone about what I've already told her? How long do you think it would take Gradoff to connect you to a widower who had also lost a three-year-old child?"

Adam didn't answer. He could send them all away and accelerate his plan, but his arm wasn't ready. His only choice was to make sure Laura stayed here and didn't go back to Kalispell until he was ready.

"Don't worry," he said firmly, "I'll make certain she won't *want* to talk about it again." Adam softened his voice. "Katherine, please be patient. You have no idea how grateful I am to you and Doc for all your help. It won't be long now. Toeless is coming up any day. He has some new information. He's good at what he does, and Ms. Duncan is evidently good at what she does, too. My shoulder actually felt better after only one treatment. Look—'' he wiggled his fingers on his right hand for her ''—hardly any pain this morning. When she comes down, would you please tell her I'll be waiting for her in here?'' He put his good arm around Katherine's thin shoulders and hugged her. "And don't worry. Everything will be all right.''

She patted his fingers, and Adam smiled at her, vowing to end this ordeal as soon as possible.

LAURA CAME DOWN the stairs a few minutes later feeling composed and professional: clean bright blue scrubs with Mountain Home Health Care stenciled on the breast pocket, hair up in a tight braid, immaculate white athletic shoes, equipment bag slung over her shoulder.

She improvised a hot pack, pouring steaming water from the kettle over a folded towel and rolling it up inside a plastic bag. Then she was ready to face her patient.

She found him in the barren front room, going over some papers at the oak table and sipping coffee from a heavy white mug. The shutters had been thrown back from all the windows, thank goodness, making the room a study in soft sunshine and glowing warm wood.

"Mr. Scott?"

He looked up with the mug poised at his lips. He was dressed in a gray sweatshirt and sweatpants, in anticipation of his treatment, she supposed, with only thick gym socks on his feet. He jerked his head toward the massage table, still folded, by the fireplace. "Doc and Katherine suggested we set the table up over there." He sipped the coffee and resumed reading the papers.

"That's nice," Laura said. She crossed the room to the bed, which Katherine had already made up. It was also Katherine, she assumed, who had placed a folded thin cotton blanket across one side.

Laura pushed on the mattress with a palm. "For now, this will be good enough. Nice and firm."

He grunted and kept reading.

She picked up the cotton blanket—it would be useful—then crossed the room and dropped her bag beside him. "You'll need to sit backward in your chair like you did yesterday."

He pushed the chair out from the table, scraping the wood floor, then flipped the chair around and sat facing away from her.

"Here." She tucked the cotton blanket over the back of the chair for his comfort. "You'll need to remove your shirt, please."

He jerked the sweatshirt up and off in one swift move, tossed it on the floor, then draped his arms over the chair back. Laura unrolled the hot pack and positioned it on his shoulder. While she waited for it to warm the muscles, she bent and dug in her bag. She pulled out a CD, positioned the player on the oak table and found the lone electrical plug in the room.

As the beat of the Pointer Sisters' "Slow Hand" filled the room, Adam gave her an irritated glance over his shoulder. "Is that really necessary?"

"Well, no," Laura admitted. "But it helps. You and I are both gonna get mighty bored with these therapy sessions. The music will keep us moving."

He shrugged and turned his back to her again.

As soon as Laura laid her hands on him, she decided she'd been wrong. There was never going to be anything boring about touching this man. She blocked out that thought and concentrated on her work.

She massaged the places where she knew the pain was lodged and wished she'd chosen a different song to start with. The beat was all right, but the words...

Having these thoughts made her a little uptight, but fortunately her hands worked automatically, and her body took up the rhythm subtly, too. Halfway through the song, she smiled as she felt Adam relax.

By the time the song was over, the muscles in Adam's back felt as fluid as a bank of shifting sand. His head rested on his forearms and his eyes were closed.

Was he asleep again? Laura wondered. Did this guy even get enough sleep? Maybe not, if he was always peering out the attic window in the middle of the night. She had to talk to him about that. If he wanted to play lookout with night-vision binoculars, he had to do it somewhere else.

"Mr. Scott?" she said softly, and he cracked his eyes in a squint at her. "Time for the second half of the treatment—the resistance training and stretching maneuvers."

Without being told he went to the massage table and lay down.

Laura got out the lotion, gave him some cross-fiber friction massage before starting the stretches. She carefully and slowly brought his arm up, then down, stretching the joint until she felt restriction. She knew how far she could push a patient, but he seemed to be getting tense too quickly. She could feel his muscles guarding, resisting her.

"You know about my wife and child," he said suddenly in the midst of a particularly difficult stretch.

"Yes," she said softly. "I was so sorry to hear that. Now you must relax, Mr. Scott."

But instead of relaxing, he twisted away from her hands and bounded up off the table, facing her, his bare chest heaving with rapid breaths. Every fiber of his body seemed tense now.

"Let's get something straight, Ms. Duncan," he said in a low voice. "My wife and child are none of your business. And if you speak about either one of them again to anyone, *ever,* I will have your license suspended for violating patient confidentiality. Is that understood?"

Laura, stunned, could barely nod before Adam turned and stomped off toward the back of the house. Again she worried: What kind of patient had she taken on?

CHAPTER FIVE

LAURA DIDN'T SEE Adam again until it was time for the afternoon treatment. She was determined to keep her mouth shut, not upset the patient and make sure this session went better than this morning's.

She was giving him a warm-up massage and hoping the music would ease the tension with this difficult patient when the front door creaked open.

The big golden dog she'd seen when she arrived yesterday sauntered into the cabin, barely giving the humans a glance. He made a sniffing patrol of the perimeter of the room before trotting happily to Adam's knee, looking at the man with a curious tilt to his black eyebrows.

Adam opened his eyes and gave the dog a lazy affectionate smile. "Morton! Where the heck have you been?"

Laura could have sworn the dog smiled back.

"Are you hungry, boy?" Adam mumbled, and let one hand drop to scratch the dog's ears.

"Who's this big guy?" Laura said in a playful voice.

Morton broke from Adam's fingers, wagging his tail as he gave Laura a curious sniff, then a frisky nudge.

"Morton! Lie down!" Adam commanded. The dog ignored him, continuing to wag his tail and gaze up at Laura. Adam sighed. "Morton's the *real* boss around this place. You'd be wise to get on his good side."

Was Mr. Scott making a little joke? Laura couldn't believe it. Maybe he was relaxing.

Morton gave her thigh another nudge as if to say, "Pet *me!*"

Laura laughed lightly and Adam eyed the dog. "He knows a good thing when he sees it," he said.

Laura laughed again, but kept her hands on her patient.

Morton finally gave up and collapsed on the floor, bringing his big head to rest on Adam's foot.

THE NEXT DAY, Laura went exploring during her free time. She climbed far up the mountainside behind the cabin, to the level where the vegetation thinned and became alpine. When the landscape finally grew barren and rocky with the altitude, she turned and followed the creek back down into the trees.

Sixteen Mile Creek ran down from the mountaintop, a trickle, a gurgle, then a riot of white water, in places as wide and deep as a river. Laura followed its course down, down, for maybe a mile or so—she couldn't really judge the distance—and came upon a densely forested area of old growth above the stone house.

She stopped, looking up at the canopy of trees. Some of them had to be eighty feet tall, with trunks so big she couldn't get her arms around them. Lodgepole pine, reaching in perfectly straight columns to the sky. Larch, fluttering their feathery leaves in the breeze. Spruce, squatting like wide sentinels.

Overcome by the beauty, Laura sat down on the ground and then, in a fit of ecstasy, threw herself onto her back on the bed of pine needles, squinting at the rays of sun that peeked through the trees.

She lay still for a while, smiling like a child enjoying a delightful secret. Then, suddenly, she had the distinct sensation of being watched.

She sat up and peered through the tree trunks toward the creek. She stood and walked a few feet onto a cornice of stone that jutted out over the water. She heard the roar of a small waterfall and peered downstream, where it tumbled over a narrow natural bridge. Her gaze lifted to a mass of huge boulders, some as big as houses, towering above on the opposite bank.

And there was Adam Scott standing, legs akimbo, on the very top of a boulder, staring down at her.

Laura wondered how long he'd been watching. The idea made her nervous. For a tense moment they stared at each other. Then Laura thought, *This is dumb. I wasn't doing anything wrong.*

"Isn't it gorgeous out here!" she shouted happily.

He nodded slowly, but there was no warmth in his squinty expression, no responding happiness.

THAT EVENING AT SUPPER, Laura observed Adam Scott closely. When he was around the Joneses, he seemed like a different man.

At the moment he was biting off the end of a sautéed asparagus spear, rolling his eyes heavenward.

"Where'd you get this dinner, Katherine? At the local drive-through?" He winked at her and she flicked a hand at him.

Laura noted again how Adam's relationship with the Joneses seemed more than neighborly.

Their ease around this table, for instance, as if they'd eaten here hundreds of times.

Tonight the room seemed less bleak. A modest fire crackled in the fireplace, illuminating the colorful counterpane quilt on the bed in the alcove. Katherine had swept and placed a checkered cloth and fat candles on the table. Doc and Adam had hauled in two stools made from sawed-off tree trunks.

"The cook always gets the credit!" Doc boomed, and plucked an asparagus spear off the platter. "I grew the blessed things."

So, Laura thought, that explains the magnificent garden.

Adam raised a wine goblet—Katherine had gone all-out, even sending Doc on the long trip down to their house to fetch crystal—and said, "Here's to you both, the wonderful cook, and the unappreciated old farmer."

Laura frowned at him. Was this man, who petted the dog, teased the cook and toasted his neighbors, the same man who'd been so gruff with her? Since the mood was relaxed, maybe this was a good time to bring up the subject of the attic bedroom. She twirled a strand of her hair, considering this while Katherine ladled a delicious-smelling soup into bowls.

There was also the sensitive subject of a bath

or shower. Before supper she'd tried to fix herself up, washed her face and brushed her hair until it made a halo around her face, but it needed a good washing.

She wondered where the shower was, wondered if there even *was* one. She was almost afraid to ask. Would he direct her to that icy creek, for heaven's sake?

"Laura?" Katherine touched her arm, trying to hand her a basket of fresh-baked whole-wheat rolls.

"Thank you." Laura folded back the napkin and lifted a roll, then passed the basket to Adam on her right, avoiding his eyes as he took it.

"I was wondering—" she directed her question to Doc and Katherine "—if you and Doc might be more comfortable in the upstairs room. That alcove seems so small." She glanced toward the antique bed crammed in there.

"That's nice of you, dear," Katherine answered, "but Doc's arthritic knees bother him. Climbing those steep stairs would aggravate his condition."

Ah, yes. Adam had told her that. Now, how could she possibly mention that she didn't appreciate Adam coming into the attic while she slept there? Maybe it wouldn't happen again.

"Anybody seen Morton today?" Doc injected cheerfully.

"He showed up to eat right on schedule," Katherine said.

"Who does Morton belong to?" Laura asked pleasantly.

"He doesn't *belong* to anybody," Doc said, after a few moments of silence. "He's very independent." His answer seemed like an evasion.

"He sprawls around wherever it suits him." Katherine raised an eyebrow at the dog, who was lying by the fireplace, soaking up warmth.

"Digs in the garden," Doc complained.

Adam finally spoke. "Actually, he's mine."

"Well, he's a great dog," Laura said, not understanding the undercurrent of emotions she sensed.

"He sure is."

She took in Adam's slightly narrowed eyes. He looked as if he was remembering something sweet—and very sad.

When dinner was over and Adam got up to leave for the stone house, Laura noticed that Morton trotted along after him. In the kitchen Katherine poured water from the big white enamel kettle into a dishpan set on the chopping block.

"This is the first time I've lived in a place without hot running water," Laura said.

"Hot water? Up here there are lots of houses that don't have it. How long have you been in Montana?"

"Four years. I trained as a physical therapist in Missoula, and of course I've done a lot of camping since I moved up here. What I mean is, I've never actually *lived* like this."

Katherine's kind eyes smiled over her reading glasses. "It is rustic, but at least Adam has a phone and electricity now. He didn't at one time. We've put a few more amenities into our house because we live there full-time. I think Adam wants to keep this place primitive."

"Where does he live when he's not up here?" *Where does he work? Why has he chosen to re-cuperate way off in the depths of a national forest?* Laura had so many questions about Adam Scott that she hardly knew where to begin.

Katherine took her time answering. She finished scraping leftovers into a large cast-iron pot—for Morton, Laura assumed.

"It's hard to say where Adam lives now. He sold his beautiful home in Seattle immediately after he lost his family. He has another one in California, but it's cold, a kind of villa. I don't care for it."

"Is that where he's from? Where he works? Seattle?"

"Oh, not really. Adam can work where he pleases. He's not tied to any one place. He has a house down in Aspen, too."

Laura was amazed. "What exactly does he do?" she pressed.

Katherine snatched up a big battered pot and put it under the tap. After two nights of rain the water pressure was high and there was quite a din as the pot filled.

"I sure made a mess cooking that big dinner. We'll need lots of hot water for scalding." She had to raise her voice to be heard. "When you've finished washing, I'll dry. I know where everything goes." She turned off the noisy tap.

Laura wanted to quiz her some more about Adam's work, but Katherine had already hefted the large pot full of water and was heading for the main room.

"This'll heat up faster in the big fireplace," she explained over her shoulder as she disappeared.

This was obviously a dodge. Why wouldn't Katherine discuss Adam's work? Laura decided to simply ask Adam about it.

"I was wondering where I could take a shower

or a bath around here," she asked when Katherine came back into the kitchen.

The older woman stopped her bustling and her mouth dropped open. "That man," she said, pursing her lips in frustration. "He didn't even think of that, I'll bet. He takes his showers in the out-of-doors down by the creek. You'll have to come to our place if you want a decent bath, dear. We've got a nice tub."

"Oh, I couldn't impose!" Laura protested.

"No imposition. We all share up here. Adam's the only one on Sixteen Mile Creek with a phone line—he shares that. Trust me, you do not want to shower in that contraption by the creek. It's attached to a tree trunk, and..." Katherine's cheeks tinted pink. "I swear. That man should have thought of this when he asked you to stay up here."

"He presumed I was going to be a guy," Laura explained.

"Well, you're not a guy, are you? Men!" Katherine huffed indignantly. "We shouldn't drive that road in the dark, but after tomorrow morning's treatment, we'll go down and you can have a nice hot bath."

While Katherine put away the last of the dishes, Laura wiped out the deep sink and looked out the bank of windows. She could see the lights of the stone house up on the mountain.

"Mr. Scott should have another treatment before he goes to bed. Is there a footpath up there?"

Katherine frowned. "More like a rocky rutted road. Hard to climb in the dark. Adam should have thought of that, too, before he took off." Katherine shook her head sadly. "It just seems like he can't stand to be around people for long. He spends most of his time alone—down the creek in the canoe, back in the woods."

"I see," Laura studied the distant yellow lights of the small stone house, thinking about the lonely man inside its walls.

"I'll have Doc go up and fetch him," Katherine said.

Laura turned from the sink. "It's no trouble for me to go up. Mr. Scott is paying me a lot of money for these treatments. I should make them convenient for him. Just give me a flashlight and point me to the path. I'll find the way."

It was slow going, carrying the clumsy arm bike and the gym bag, but Laura made steady progress.

To ward off the evening chill, she'd pulled an oversize white cable-knit sweater over her T-shirt and tucked her dark gray stretch pants into thick oatmeal-colored socks and brown hiking boots.

But as she climbed the steep path, she wished she hadn't dressed so snugly. She felt a flush of anticipation as she got closer to the small stone house high up on the mountain—and to the man who had retreated into it.

CHAPTER SIX

WHEN SHE WAS HALFWAY UP the steep, rocky path, Morton padded out of the trees to greet her. She shifted her burdens and reached down to scratch the dog's ears.

"At least somebody's glad to see me," she muttered. "I sure wish you could talk, big fella. I bet you'd tell me what the heck's going on around this joint."

The stone house sat on the edge of a small clearing rimmed with towering fragrant spruce trees that seemed to be reaching for the moon. When she stepped into the moonlit oval, Morton bounded ahead, barking a greeting. Well, so much for worrying about announcing herself.

The plank door opened a crack and a bright light came on, nearly blinding Laura. "Ms. Duncan?" Adam's irritated voice spoke from behind the beacon.

Laura shielded her eyes. "Mr. Scott, I'm here for your evening exercises." She lowered the heavy gym bag, and Morton seated himself on his haunches at her feet.

"Oh." The light snapped off and the door swung open. "I could have come down to the main house."

When her eyes adjusted, she focused on the figure silhouetted in the doorway. "No need. I should have reminded you about it. We can work here—for tonight. If that's agreeable to you."

"Uh. Sure." But he sounded *un*sure.

When Laura bent to pick up the gym bag, Adam rushed forward. "I can take that."

"And tear up your shoulder?" Laura admonished, then hitched the bag over her own shoulder and walked ahead of him.

She stepped inside and was surprised. The interior of the stone house was as warm and beautiful as the big cabin down the mountain was cold and ugly.

The stone walls were high, and framed prints—pretty pictures of flowers mostly—were arranged in artful groups.

The windows, deep-set and multipaned, had thick wooden frames. The pine floors were varnished to a high gloss and covered with cozy braided rugs. A simple mission-style couch and two matching side chairs were covered in dark supple leather.

But otherwise the place was a mess, strewn with Adam's discarded clothes, papers, empty pop cans. His personal grooming was so meticulous that she would never have pegged him for a slob.

The small room was softly lit by a crackling fire and, on a low chest by the bed, an old-fashioned kerosene lamp. The rumpled quilts on the pole-style bed looked like he might have been resting.

But the screen of a laptop computer glowed from the bedside table. Katherine had said there was no electricity up here, so the thing was obviously running on batteries.

Adam darted around her and snapped it shut.

Laura cleared her throat. "We need to get started right away while this moist heat pack is still hot." She turned her back to him, dropped the gym bag on the couch and opened it. "We'll need a chair and blanket as usual."

He disappeared into an adjoining room and came back strong-arming a straight-backed chair. He set it facing the fire, grabbed a throw off the couch and folded it over the back.

Then he faced Laura and raised one eyebrow while unbuttoning his shirt. "You know," he said pleasantly as he yanked the shirt off his broad shoulders, "these treatments are already helping."

Laura glanced around the room nervously, suddenly wishing for a less intimate atmosphere. Something along the lines of the clinical fluorescent lights and bare tile floors in the physical therapy room back at the Kalispell clinic.

"Well, I...I want you to get your money's worth."

That was a really lame thing to say, she thought as she set the arm bike in place on the coffee table. A transparent attempt to remind him—and herself—that this was a professional relationship, albeit an unusual one. And why would she need to remind either of them of that?

But minutes later, when she touched him, she knew exactly why.

His skin was warm after the heat pack, and his wonderful scent was quickly becoming familiar to her—too familiar. And there was that unmistakable charge in her fingertips, something she had never felt while touching any other patient...or any other man, for that matter.

As she dug her thumbs into his tight shoulder muscles, he sighed.

Deciding that now, while he was relaxed, might be a good time to bring up the subject of her leaving again, she said carefully, "I called

Mountain Home Health today and asked them to start looking for a therapist to replace me.''

He tensed and gave her a sharp glance over his shoulder. "I don't understand why that's necessary," he said crossly.

Laura had no intention of telling him why she thought it was necessary. "Time to use the arm bike," she said briskly.

He stood up and faced her, but didn't move toward the coffee table. He looked at her intensely, assessing her with that dark-eyed scrutiny that made her uncomfortable. "I told you I don't want another therapist," he said flatly.

"Or maybe we could try the finger ladder. You just walk your fingers up and down, and that helps you raise your arm higher and higher. I'll show you." She reached for the gym bag, and pulled out a miniature ladder. "See?"

When she began to demonstrate, he put his hand out and gently stilled hers. "I don't want another therapist," he repeated.

Laura turned toward the fire, trying not to look at him. Out of the corner of her eye she could see his broad chest, could see him taking in and releasing a deep breath as if he was preparing for a speech. He was.

"Look," he began quietly, "I started to ask you to leave the other day because I didn't think it would work to have such an attractive woman for a therapist.''

She glanced at him, shocked at his honesty.

''It was nothing against you—it was just not what I thought I needed right now. But then when you told me you had decided to leave—it sounds irrational I guess—I realized I wanted you, not some other therapist. You really are skilled, Ms. Duncan, maybe the best. And I need the best. I must have a functioning shoulder as soon as possible.''

At her questioning frown, he said, ''I have my reasons. But it's obvious that something about this situation is making you very uncomfortable.'' He stopped, turned to her. ''Isn't there some way we can continue with these treatments without making each other uncomfortable?''

It was the most he'd said to her since she'd arrived. She was surprised by his candor, and as much as she wanted to deny everything he'd just said, she couldn't. All of it was true. She *was* uncomfortable, except she couldn't possibly admit the reason the way he just had.

But now, with his honesty, Laura felt it was possible to stay. Maybe they could work together for the full six weeks.

''All right, I'll stay.''

He released a breath. ''Thank you. Of course,

between treatments you're free to spend your time any way you please.''

''I appreciate that,'' Laura said.

She hadn't thought much about how she would occupy the hours between treatments. Six weeks was a long time. But if what Katherine had said about Adam Scott's solitary habits was true, surely she wouldn't have to see that much of him.

THE NEXT MORNING, Adam suggested that they set up the massage table in the stone house. He didn't say why, but Laura guessed that he didn't want Doc or Katherine to walk in on the workouts.

Between the two of them, with Adam using his good arm, they managed to lug the folded table up the path.

Laura was surprised at how different the little stone house looked by daylight. By firelight it had seemed dark, cozy, cocoonlike. But flooded with sunshine—the deep-set windows were bare—the varnished wood floor glimmered brightly around the richly patterned rugs, and all the colors—the burgundy leather of the mission furniture, the framed prints of wildflowers, the collection of antique colored-glass bottles on a windowsill—seemed brighter, cheerier. Too bad

Adam Scott wasn't. He endured the workout in silence, then disappeared into the woods.

After the treatment Laura and Katherine took Doc's old green Suburban down to the elderly couple's house.

Laura was delighted when she saw the house, A two-story saltbox full of windows, capped with a bright-blue standing-ridge roof. An antique, Katherine proudly informed Laura, built just after the turn of the century. Pale-yellow tongue-and-groove siding alternated with white casement windows that rolled open and pressed aside low pine branches.

Katherine led Laura through the dewy grass and up a flagstone path to the front door which had a real leaded-glass window. She inserted a key and the hinges creaked musically as the door swung open.

Unlike Adam, Katherine and Doc did not live like dour recluses. Just as Laura had guessed, they lived more like superannuated hippies. Plants sprouting over the sides of macramé hangers. A weaving loom. A quilting rack. An upright piano. Books and pictures and clutter and old comfy chairs. Every detail communicated the care, conservation and celebration of a long and happy marriage.

"I love your house!" Laura exclaimed.

"It's comfortable," Katherine allowed modestly.

Katherine built a fire in the potbellied stove, then filled the claw-foot tub in the bathroom to the brim with bubbles and steaming hot water.

"I've got chores," she said, "so enjoy your bath." She closed the door.

Laura assessed the room as she slipped out of her sweats and laid them on a bench made from a split log, rubbed smooth by years of use.

She grasped the edge of the tub and lowered herself into the water. She used to take baths like this at Gran's farm. The feeling of being back there enveloped her as she sank to her chin and closed her eyes.

Even the smells were the same: the faint odor of the propane as the hot-water heater kicked on, the sweet soapy fragrance and the pungent pine cleanser.

Smoothing the suds up her arm, she thought about how her mother, Nadine, used to shuttle her off to Gran's farm every summer so Nadine and her self-centered third husband, Lyle, could pretend their life was not complicated by a child from a previous marriage.

After her first summer on the small farm near Wylie—climbing the huge old pecan trees, exploring the aging farm buildings, eating Gran's simple daily fare—Laura hadn't wanted to go back to Dallas.

She had to go back of course, only to endure Nadine's bizarre combination of suffocating concern and benign neglect. But every summer Laura could count on staying with Gran.

Years later Laura had tried to convince her wealthy husband to pay Nadine's price and buy the old farm, but Stuart had flatly refused. It was, he said, a "poor investment."

Strangers lived on the place now.

A tear seeped out from under Laura's closed eyelids. "No matter, Gran," she whispered. "I sort of found my way back to you, anyway, didn't I? At least in my heart."

AFTER HER BATH, Laura and Katherine puttered around the place companionably. They picked a big crock of ripe cherries from Katherine's trees. To make cherry jelly, Katherine said. Then they baked some oat-bran muffins to go with the soup Katherine had put on to simmer that morning.

"Heavens! It's later than I thought," Laura said when she checked her watch. "Hope I'll be able to get Adam's afternoon treatment started on time." She gave Katherine a worried glance.

"Don't you worry about that." They climbed

into the Suburban, and Katherine threw the truck into gear. "There's always the shortcut."

Just beyond the entrance to Doc and Katherine's house, the shortcut veered upward off Sixteen Mile Creek Road like a scar slashing up the side of the mountain, little more than a rutted wash. Katherine drove it like a white-haired demon. Up, up the rocky path, making the cherries bounce around in the crock in Laura's lap.

But, as she'd promised, Katherine got Laura back to the cabin in time for the afternoon treatment, conducted up in the stone house to the beat of Fleetwood Mac's "Dreams."

After supper, when she and Katherine were in the kitchen washing up pots and pans and soup bowls, they heard the wind outside kicking up. The single naked lightbulb above their heads flickered.

"That is so annoying," Katherine complained as she set aside the steaming kettle. She reached for a kerosene lamp and took it down. "The power lines up here are really unstable. These big tree limbs are always whacking them." She struck a match just as the room went black.

"Power's out!" they heard Doc's voice call out cheerfully from the main room where he and Adam were stacking firewood and building a fire.

According to the radio, the temperature was

supposed to drop tonight. The timbers of the old cabin creaked and the windows rattled, as if protesting the sudden shift in the weather.

Standing there in the flickering light of the match flame, Laura thought she heard something—a faint rapping noise.

"Did you hear that?" she asked, and cocked her head.

Katherine held the match to the wick of the lamp and adjusted the flame. "No, I didn't." The soft yellow light created a circle of security in the room.

"It sounded like someone knocking."

"Knocking? On the back door?"

Laura wasn't sure, it didn't make sense that anyone would climb the narrow flagstone path all the way around to the back door in the dark.

"It didn't sound like knocking, exactly," Laura tiptoed to the door and looked out the small window into the darkness. "It was more of a tapping." She framed her eyes with her palms, trying to see past the screen into the darkness.

"Could be a hummingbird feeder hitting the window," Katherine was saying when suddenly Laura screamed and staggered backward.

She knocked the pans off the chopping block

and the crock, too, sending cherries bouncing away like marbles.

Adam and Doc appeared instantly, Adam wielding a gun.

Doc slipped on the cherries and Adam grabbed for the old man with his weak arm while he kept the gun trained on the door. "What is it?" he demanded.

Laura had landed on her rear among the cherries. She let out one incoherent yelp, then said, "It's a man!"

Adam silently signaled them all to get down. Doc and Katherine crouched with Laura behind the chopping block.

Adam doused the lamp and plastered himself beside the door. He carefully turned his head to peek out into the darkness, then jerked the door open in disgust. "Toeless," he said calmly, "get your ass in here."

"Good God." Laura felt Katherine slump with relief. "It's just that Toeless person."

"Toeless?" Laura echoed as she struggled to her feet.

"Yes, Toeless." Katherine gave Laura a reassuring pat. "Everything's all right. He's just a bit strange, not dangerous." Doc found a match and relit the lamp.

A large muscular man had come through the

kitchen door. He was smiling. He tipped his greasy baseball cap to Katherine deferentially. "Ma'am. Very nice to see you again."

He was indeed strange. He wore a black eye patch over his right eye. That was what had really spooked Laura when she'd looked out—a man peering at her with one eye. His silver-streaked hair was slicked straight back into a bushy ponytail. He had on a camouflage jacket that looked as if it had actually seen war, and his faded patched jeans were tucked into knee-high silver-studded black boots. He glanced around at the others, one eyebrow raised. "Seems I've caused a little disturbance."

"You nearly gave this child a heart attack." Katherine's indignation was obvious as she snatched up the pan near her feet.

"Sorry about that. As soon as the lady freaked, I backed away." He glanced at Adam. "I was looking for you."

Adam flicked the safety on the gun, then tucked the weapon into the back of his belt. "Ms. Duncan—" he jerked a thumb at the big man "—this is Toeless Elko."

The man removed his baseball cap and held it over his heart. "At your service, ma'am."

"Mr. Elko, I'm sorry I screamed," Laura said, the residue of fright accentuating her Texas accent, "but you scared the daylights outta me." She brushed at her pants.

"Call me Toeless, ma'am. Everybody does."

"They call him that because he chopped off his own toe with an ax," Katherine said.

For a second Adam looked as if he might actually grin. Then he leaned against the counter with his legs crossed at the ankles and his arms folded over his chest, shaking his head. "Toeless, this lady is my physical therapist."

"Laura Duncan." Laura extended her still-trembling hand.

Toeless took it. "Nice to meet you, ma'am." His large paw held Laura's fingers gently. He didn't act as rough as he looked. "I'm so sorry I frightened you."

"Toeless is a logger who comes up every so often to help me with projects I can't handle because of my shoulder." Adam explained. He pushed himself off the counter. "You look pale. You'd better sit down." He took Laaura's elbow and steered her toward the stool.

"Wait. Don't sit..." Katherine covered her lips with her fingers as if suppressing a smile.

Adam looked behind Laura, then rolled his eyes. "Hold it."

He reached around to knock something from the seat of her pants, then stopped abruptly. He was actually blushing. "Uh…you have a bunch of cherries…there."

Laura twisted to look at her backside. Several smashed cherries were stuck to her pants.

She bit her lip and felt her own cheeks turning pink. "Well, heavens, this is no way to make cherry jelly," she joked, and plucked at the pulpy mess. When she started to laugh, Doc and Katherine chuckled along with her.

Adam grinned crookedly, then coughed and bent to pick up the broken crockery pieces.

"I assume you'll be staying a few days, Toeless. As usual." Katherine had stopped laughing. Now she sounded irritated as she stooped beside Adam to clean up the cherries.

"Yes, ma'am. I sure appreciate the invitation," Toeless said. "I've got my tent in the truck. I'll camp up the mountain a ways, if that's all right."

"Perfectly okay," Doc said. "On occasion I've wanted to move up there myself."

Katherine gave Doc a withering look and took a handful of cherries to the trash.

Toeless turned to Laura with a twinkle in his eye. "Again, I'm real sorry I spooked you, ma'am and caused your pretty jeans to get all messed up."

Adam gave Toeless a droll glance before he asked Laura, "Are you okay now?"

She smiled and nodded.

"Where's your Land Rover?" Adam asked Toeless. "We didn't hear anything."

"Blew a tire about half a mile down Sixteen Mile Creek. I hate that damned road. I thought I'd better come up to the back door—you told me Doc and Katherine were using the front room as a bedroom. I didn't want to disturb them."

Katherine shook her head.

"Let's go do something about that tire," Adam said as he reached into a drawer for a flashlight. The two men went outside.

When they were gone, the image of Adam with that gun burned in Laura's mind. Of course, people who lived in remote places could be expected to need some protection, but the way he had obviously had it at the ready bothered her. "What kind of project are they working on?" Laura tried to sound casual as she resumed drying the dishes.

Katherine stopped wiping the chopping block. She tilted her head back, eyes closed, too dramatic a pose for such a simple question.

"Katherine?"

The woman sighed. "I don't like it when Toeless comes around. He's trouble."

She went back to scrubbing the wood with fervor. "As for their 'project'... Well, let's just say it's better if you don't know."

CHAPTER SEVEN

WHEN THE SUN CAME UP, Laura looked out from her upstairs window and saw a brand-new white Land Rover parked beside her Toyota. Such an expensive vehicle, she thought, fit this Toeless person about like a tutu fit a bull. There was something more than strange about that guy, about this whole situation, something Katherine obviously didn't approve of.

During the morning treatment Laura skipped the music. She had questions to ask.

"What do you do for a living, Mr. Scott?" she got right to it during the cross-friction massage.

His muscles immediately tensed under her fingers. "I'm a scientist."

"That's interesting." *And vague,* she added to herself. "What kind of scientist?"

"A botanist. Can we just get on with the treatment?" he said irritably. "What happened to the music?"

She put on a CD and finished the workout in silence.

After she returned to the main house, Laura decided to help Doc in the garden. Maybe she'd have more luck getting information out of him.

The late-morning sun was glorious. As she walked down the path toward him, Doc stopped hoeing and waved a friendly greeting. He was wearing his usual straw hat and a pair of stained overalls over a faded purple T-shirt.

"Would you like some help?" she called out.

"A gardener can always use an apprentice," he replied.

The neat rows of vegetables were practically exploding with produce. "I can't believe you can grow such beautiful broccoli up here." Laura pointed at the lush plants as she approached him. "My grandmother tried growing broccoli in Texas once. But the sun cooked it before it was picked."

Doc smiled as he pulled a kerchief from the pocket of his overalls. He removed his straw hat and mopped his brow.

"It's a lot of work, but I do it to help Adam. Today I'm hoeing a few weeds, then I need to pull the last of those onions." He pointed at a big basket near some tall onion plants, some of which had already gone to seed.

Laura held out her arms. "I'm here to help."

She'd admired Doc's garden during her explorations the day before, but she hadn't actually worked in a vegetable garden since her childhood days, helping Gran dig potatoes and cut scratchy okra.

This garden was indeed different from the dry land farms in Texas. The soil, rich and loamy, fell away from the onions in one gentle shake. Before long the earthy smell transported Laura, relaxed her.

After she'd put a few onions in the basket, she started her usual chattering.

"This is a mighty big garden. I don't see how you get all this work done around here. I noticed you've even got enough dry tamarack wood laid out behind the shed for three winters."

"Like I said, I want to help Adam," Doc replied, then continued to work in silence.

Laura wondered about that. Why were Doc and Katherine so concerned with Adam's welfare? Of course, he was a lonely widower, but even so, their attitude seemed overly solicitous.

After a while Laura took a breather and stood up. "I'd forgotten how much I love gardens!" she exclaimed.

Doc straightened, too. "Yes. Gardens have a

universal appeal. I think it's because they're quiet.''

Oops! Laura thought. *Is that a hint that I'm talking too much?*

"I didn't mean," Doc said as if he'd read her mind, "that I don't enjoy human conversation." He bent, steadily pulling onions as he talked. "I meant that plants have their own silent generous language. And plant lovers share a common bond, too, a common language, if you will."

Laura nodded her understanding. "Katherine said you're a botanist. Adam told me he's one, too. Is that how you all came to know each other? Through your work?"

Doc looked uncomfortable. He focused doggedly on pulling onions. "Yes…" he answered with some hesitation. "It was our work that first brought us together."

"Your work must have been fascinating."

He glanced over his shoulder and smiled. "Yes. And challenging. I was even privileged to spend some time in the Chelsea Physic Garden in London, England. My personal interest is herbalism—the whole plant." Doc's hesitation disappeared as he began to talk freely about something he obviously loved. "But of course my…employers were always more interested in the pharmacology—extracts of one principle of a plant.'' He tossed a few onions in the basket. ''And I like to think that the travel was good for my family. My little girl could speak three languages before she finished grade school.''

When he stopped speaking, Laura said, ''I didn't know you had a daughter. Where does she live?''

Doc looked down at the onion plants in his hand, but Laura sensed he wasn't seeing them. His forehead creased and he suddenly looked as if he might cry. Laura had the terrible feeling she'd harmed him just by asking these simple questions.

''Laura, I cannot tell you certain things. And yet there are certain things…but it would not do you any good to know. I'm sorry.''

''No, I'm the one who's sorry—for asking personal questions,'' she said. ''Tell me about your and Adam's work? It sounds fascinating.''

At her mention of Adam's name, Doc straightened and stared off toward the cabin, his weathered face as still as carved tamarack.

''Doc, am I prying again? I'm sorry. I guess I'm just worried that something is going on up here. I get the feeling there's something…out of control about Adam's situation.''

Doc gave a gravelly little chuckle. ''Out of control. My dear, you are very perceptive, but

then of course, all of life is out of our control.''
He gestured with the head of an onion as if aiming a scepter at a kingdom. "This entire beautiful garden, for example, could be destroyed by Mother Nature in one instant. Anything can be taken from us. Anything."

"I suppose so," Laura agreed quietly. "My gran always said that even your own life is not a certainty."

"Things more precious than your own life can be taken from you," Doc said sadly.

Laura knew that now he was talking about something besides this garden. Adam? His little girl? And then it hit her. Little girls grow up, don't they? Laura thought about the look in Katherine's eyes when she'd told her about Adam's wife and child being killed.

She gave Doc's shoulder a friendly pat. "I must've turned into a sissy since my gardening days with Gran. Seems to me it's getting pretty warm out here." She squinted at the midday sun, bent to pick up the huge basket of onions.

"Let me get that, Laura," Doc said, reaching for the basket.

"I'm okay," Laura touched his arm. "Now. Where do you suggest we wash these? Down in Hell Freezes Over Creek?"

Doc laughed.

FROM HIS SECLUDED PLACE among the boulders, Adam watched Laura's graceful movements as she bent to pick up the basket. Doc took two steps forward to take it himself, but she stopped him with a gentle touch on the arm. Then he saw the old man throw back his head and laugh.

Man. It had been a long time since he'd seen Doc laugh like that. The familiar snake of guilt twisted in his gut.

Laura said something else and tilted her head saucily, her answering laugh echoing musically in the mountain air. Adam wished he could have made out her words. *If you want to talk to the woman, why don't you just go ahead and talk to her?* he chided himself. The answer was obvious, at least to him. *And let her make you laugh, too?* And let her distract him from the one thing he had to do. The one thing he had to do if he was ever going to be able to look in the mirror again.

Mind back on his task, he surveyed his surroundings. This spot wouldn't work—although from here it would be easy to pick off any unwelcome visitors as they reached the end of Sixteen Mile Creek Road. He could shoot out a tire with one arrow and nock another before anyone had a chance to exit the vehicle. But there were too many near-at-hand places to run for cover. The clearing at the top of the path leading to the stone house was still the prime spot. As for luring the target that far up the mountain, Toeless would have some ideas.

THE NEXT DAY, Katherine came to the back door and called out, "Laww-ra! Would you mind telling Adam and Toeless that lunch is ready?"

Laura, who'd been in the garden, began to make her way up to the stone house. But as she rounded a bend in the path, she heard the men's voices carrying clearly through the still mountain air. She cut through the woods toward the sound, picking her way over the verdant cushion of ferns and pine needles.

About fifty yards below the path, she spotted Toeless and Adam through the tree trunks. They were sitting atop the cornice of rock that jutted out toward the river. Some kind of equipment—archers' bows?—was stacked between them on the rock.

Below their high perch the mountainside veered sharply down for another thirty yards into the creek below. Now Laura could hear the steady rhythm of rushing water, as well as the mens' voices.

She struggled to find her footing and was about to call out when something Adam said stopped her.

"You mean the guys who ran our van off the mountain?" he demanded angrily.

Laura stiffened.

"It checks out," Toeless said.

"And Gradoff—he's in the States with them?"

"Left Russia two days ago. Landed in L.A."

"Seems like he could've had his goons eliminate me without coming over personally."

Laura's heart raced. What on earth? *Russia? Eliminate him?* She hesitated, unsure whether to turn back or break in on this awful conversation.

For several seconds there was no sound except the rushing stream, and Laura seized the chance to make her presence known.

"Mr. Scott?" she called out as she made her way down the slope. Both men turned to look at her, then stood.

"Katherine asked me to come and fetch you for lunch." Laura came to a halt in the small clearing above the cornice. She eyed the archery equipment at the men's feet. The bows were the kind that looked like molded plastic camouflage material and the arrows were aluminum.

Adam and Toeless exchanged looks, and Toeless said, "I'll have to pass on lunch. Please give Katherine my apologies. Talk to you later,

Adam.'' He jumped down off the boulders and began climbing the rocky slope toward the path.

''Did I say something wrong?'' Laura asked.

''No. He's got work to do.''

Adam and Laura stood looking at each other with open suspicion. ''Are those bows and arrows?'' she said inanely. What she meant was, *I hope you're not using archery equipment with that bad shoulder.*

He squinted at her. ''No. They're knitting needles. Toeless and I are making an afghan.''

Laura's cheeks grew warm and her lips became pinched. But along with her frustration, she felt a twinge of fear. She didn't know anything about this man. ''Katherine has your lunch ready,'' she said quietly, and turned to go.

He leaped off the boulder and grabbed her upper arm in his strong left hand. ''Forget lunch! What did you overhear?''

Laura's cheeks grew hotter. ''What do you mean?''

''Coming down the path just now. I know how sound carries on this mountain.'' His grip tightened. ''Tell me.''

''Mr. Scott, please,'' she whispered. He released her arm, but he continued to pin her with his dark gaze.

''Ms. Duncan.'' He planted his hands on his

belt and studied the tops of the tall pines around them for a moment. When he looked back down at her, his eyes were calmer, kinder. "Ms. Duncan, listen. You arrived just as Toeless and I were having a very serious discussion. You see, Toeless Elko isn't a logger. He's my lifelong friend and he's...he's also my private investigator."

Laura blinked and tried not to look shocked.

"He's here to help me solve a...a serious business problem. Now, please, I must know. What did you hear?"

"Not much," Laura said. "Really."

His smile was both sad and patient. "I know how strange this situation seems to you. And I know what a nice person you are." His smile widened at her confused frown. "I had Toeless investigate you."

Laura sucked in a breath. Adam Scott had her investigated? "What is going on up here?" she demanded.

"You don't need to know. I'm the one paying *you,* remember?"

"You aren't paying me enough to be involved in something dangerous!" she countered.

"If you didn't hear anything just now, what makes you suspect my business is dangerous?"

Laura pointed at the archery equipment. "That

stuff sure looks dangerous. Is that why you need your shoulder fixed? To use that thing?'' She gave the bow a hostile nudge with her toe.

''Would it matter? Isn't it your job to get me well regardless of what I want to do? Now—I need to know what you heard.''

Laura puffed out her lips in a huge sigh. ''All right. I heard you say something about Russia. And—'' she could hardly bring herself to say it ''—and about somebody running your van off a mountain.''

He nodded as if he'd figured as much. His expression turned faraway and sad, and when his silence became unbearable, she added, ''Is that how it happened?''

He looked at her, his face now a mask. ''We're not going to talk about that. Apparently you heard too much. Do you have a family back in Kalispell?''

She raised her chin, though the question was disquieting. ''You should already know the answer if you've had me investigated.''

He smiled, warmly this time. ''We'd only gotten as far as your job credentials. Toeless was about to give me a full report when the subject of it walked up.''

''Oh. Well, I'm so sorry for the interruption. You know, you could have just asked *me* about my background and saved yourself some money.''

"The investigation is nothing against you. I just can't take any chances right now.''

There it was again. The implication of danger. Laura decided that she didn't have anything to hide. She answered his original question. "I don't have any family here, but I have a lot of friends.''

"You aren't from this area, are you? Isn't that a Texas accent?''

Laura wondered what Toeless would eventually tell him. "Yes, I'm from Dallas originally.''

"Dallas? What brought you to a place where there are fewer than four people per square mile?''

"The fact that there are fewer than four people per square mile.'' She smiled and was relieved to see a wry smile in response.

"Yeah. They say Montana is a state with wide margins,'' he said so agreeably that Laura relaxed some.

"After I left my husband,'' she explained, "I just wanted peace, a remote place to start my life over. I found a physical therapy school up here—it's what I'd always wanted to do—and after a while Montana began to feel like home.''

"I see.'' His eyes became piercing, serious

again. "Ms. Duncan, all I ask is that you not discuss anything you've seen or heard up here with your friends back in Kalispell."

"My friends are mostly at Mountain Home Health, and they have a copy of your chart."

"But the fact that I lost a child isn't on that chart. Nor is there anything about Russians—" he gave her a sharp look "—or the fact that somebody ran our van off the mountain. Part of the reason I'm willing to pay you such a high salary to do the therapy way up here is to maintain a certain...privacy."

You mean secrecy, Laura thought, but she said. "I always maintain patient confidentiality."

"That's all I ask. That, and a rapid recovery."

"How fast we progress is up to you. Normally it would take longer, much longer, to make a change in tissue that's been neglected. You're lucky, you know, you didn't..." Aware that she was lecturing, Laura stopped herself. "Well, six weeks is really pushing it," she finished quietly.

"I may not even have that much time," he mumbled.

"Pardon?"

"Nothing."

"The speed with which patients recover depends largely on how motivated they are."

"Trust me, I'm very motivated." He snatched

up the bows in his left hand, and the arrows in his right. She noticed that his grip was much stronger than it had been only a few days ago. "Tell Katherine I'll be down for lunch shortly."

"So you aren't going to tell me what this is all about, what those things are for?" She pointed at the archery equipment.

He stopped and cut a glance back at her. "My plans don't concern you."

"Yes, they do!" she called after him as he turned away again, "if I'm helping you do something illegal."

He stopped and squinted down at her. "Illegal? What about justice, Ms. Duncan? But, like I said, my plans don't concern you. I know exactly what I'm doing, and why I'm doing it."

LATER THAT AFTERNOON when Adam was certain Laura had gone to Katherine's house for a bath, he and Toeless met again on the rock cornice.

"With a student visa, Toly Gradoff will have more freedom of movement," Toeless continued his report. "It'll be harder to track him now— my contacts won't do me much good."

"We don't have to find them, anyway. They'll find me. Remember, I'm still what they want."

Toeless nodded. "But we've got to be ready when they do find you."

"I'll be ready." Adam rolled the vicious-looking steel-pronged arrow tip in his palm.

"And what if they kill you first?"

Adam shook his head. "They can't just kill me. It has to look like an accident for them to collect. That was their original plan—to have me die in a car accident."

Toeless nodded. "Right. Properly dead, you'd be a double value—worth two million dollars as the key man of the company and unable to go to the authorities about the laundered money."

Adam smiled ruefully. "I'd be such a useful corpse." His expression grew cold. "It doesn't matter what happens to me, anyway. As long as I avenge my wife and child's deaths."

Toeless looked instantly sad, but he covered the painful moment. "Well, hey, buddy, but what about old Toeless's ass? And what about the Joneses? And your little therapist? What about her? Other people could get hurt in this deal."

Adam's head snapped around to face him. Other people *could* get hurt? Other people *had* been hurt! Only Toeless could get away with saying something like that to him now. "I am not about to let anybody else get hurt. That's why we're waiting. The therapy should be complete in five weeks. Then she'll leave. Doc and Katherine will head down the mountain, or even back to Seattle, the minute I tell them to."

"Five weeks. That's a gamble—who finds who first."

"If they do find me sooner than I want them to…" There was another stretching silence, emphasized by the sound of rushing water. "If they do, your job is to get Doc and Katherine and…Ms. Duncan out of here."

"Let's hope it doesn't come to that."

"If it weren't for this shoulder, I wish to hell those bastards *would* find me right now. Today. That's all I want—just them and me. Alone up here. The sooner the better."

"Yeah, but you *do* have the shoulder. What about the therapist? How much did she hear?"

"Enough." Adam sighed. "She thinks I'm getting ready to do something illegal."

"Well, aren't you?"

"Don't go soft on me."

"Don't go *dead* on *me*."

"Not a chance. This—" Adam held up a pod, which looked like a tiny red balloon filled with fluid "—contains enough stuff to fell an elephant, and it works from a great distance."

"You didn't tell *her* any of this, did you?

"No." Adam sighed. "But she's suspicious, and she sure as hell complicates things."

"In more ways than one? She's a pretty little thing."

Adam gave Toeless a wry glance. "I can see that for myself. But that's not what I'm paying you to tell me."

Toeless sighed. "Okay, wiseass. She's been out of physical-therapy school for about six months. Whizzed through. Straight A's.

"Churchgoing. Clean credit record. Apparently not involved in a serious relationship—at least for the past four years. Before that, it gets interesting. Originally she's from Dallas. Rich man's ex-wife. A guy named Stuart Hayden Crestwood. That part's a little strange. You know, why would a rich girl from Dallas move all the way to this northern backcountry?"

So far this story jibed with everything Laura had told Adam about herself, except she hadn't mentioned that her ex-husband was rich. "And?"

"She left the guy with a giant plastic bill and cleaned out a sizable investment account."

She'd conveniently left out that part, too.

"She was not nice about it, Adam. If I was a rich guy like *you,* I wouldn't get involved with her...you know, romantically."

"Romantically? Elko, you are such a hopeless reprobate when it comes to women." Another silence. "Besides, I told you—" his voice was serious now, low "—I'm through with romance. After what I had with Elizabeth—"

"Elizabeth would be mad as hell if she could see how you're living now. How you've changed. How you've shut yourself off. If she could hear you—"

"But she can't, can she?" Adam jumped to his feet. "Elizabeth…can't…hear…me." He balled his hands into fists and let his voice rise. "She can't hear me because she's dead! And my baby girl's dead with her!"

"Adam—"

But the monster of Adam's anger had suddenly roared to the surface. "What I do now, how I live my life," he shouted, "is nobody's business but my own. And if I don't need love, don't *want* love, that is my business." Adam jabbed a finger at his own chest. "Isn't it? Isn't it?" he demanded. But he didn't wait for Toeless to answer. He turned and started climbing up and into the forest.

Toeless stood up on the boulder. "Adam, wait!" he called out. "I loved Elizabeth and

Anna, too! Adam! Dammit!'' Toeless's pleading voice echoed off the trees as Adam disappeared into the woods.

CHAPTER EIGHT

LAURA STUDIED Toeless's back as he adjusted a tent stake. A logger? Right. Exactly as she'd suspected, he was not what he appeared to be. Nothing, no one, in this place was.

Whoever these people might be, Laura reminded herself, she must remember to treat everyone with professional detachment. That was her role, the visiting professional. But the next five weeks would be a lot less nerve-racking if she had a better idea of what Adam Scott was all about.

Then again, maybe not.

"Mr. Elko?" she called softly as she walked toward his tent.

He turned. His unpatched eye widened, then crinkled as he smiled. "Ms. Duncan. Where'd you come from?"

She stopped beside one of the folding camp stools he'd placed in front of the tent. "I was out for a walk and spotted you. Please. Call me Laura."

He smiled. "Okay. But only if you'll call me Toeless."

"Any relation to Shoeless Joe Jackson?"

Toeless chuckled at her little joke and took a seat on one of the stools. "You like baseball?"

"I'm a casual fan."

He gestured and she sat down on the other stool.

"I did therapy on a minor-league player a while back. He had a vacation cabin up near Glacier. Gave me a free baseball education. Patients talk a lot during therapy. Speaking of therapy, I'm looking for Adam. Do you know where he is?"

"He was pretty mad at me the last time I saw him." Toeless's voice sounded sad. He scanned the ridge of trees higher on the mountain, nodding. "He headed up there."

Laura longed to ask what had upset Adam, but she decided to take this one step at a time. "Well, I guess I can't give him a treatment if I can't find him." She spread her arms wide. "This spot is sure gorgeous!"

"That's why I pitched my tent here." Toeless smiled.

Below their vantage point, the big creek wound like a sparkling ribbon, tumbling in frothy caps over large stones, then turning into a sheet of clear green as it flowed over the narrow falls where matching boulders formed a natural bridge. Far below Laura could see the cornice of rock where she'd come upon Toeless and Adam talking earlier that day. On the opposite bank

towered the large boulders where Adam had
stood a couple of days before. Beyond those rose
the small meadow bordered by clusters of fir,
spruce and pine.

"I have never seen wildflowers growing that
thick. So much bitterroot. And look!" Laura
pointed across at the tall plants with golden-
yellow clusters of delicate orchid-like blooms.
"Butter-and-eggs—my very favorite."

"You know, that's Adam's spot." Toeless
pointed at the large boulders across the creek.
"He goes there to think."

"To think or to brood?"

Toeless arched his eyebrows at Laura. "Tell
me something. You said people talk during therapy. How about Adam? Does he talk to you during therapy?"

"I wouldn't repeat any of it if he did, but
mostly he's quiet. Doc told me he wanted to get
his shoulder in shape so he could go fly-fishing
again." Laura thought how *she* was the one who
was fishing now, but she refused to feel guilty.
What if she really was in danger? Didn't she
have a right to know?

Toeless didn't reply. He folded his arms across
his chest and stared off at the swirling white water thirty feet below, his mouth set in a grim line.

Laura cleared her throat. "He has something besides fly-fishing in mind, doesn't he."

Toeless turned to her. In his one eye Laura thought she read something new. Fear. Or warning. "But he didn't tell *you* that."

"No." Laura had never cared for duplicity. "But I know there's something weird going on. For example—" she proceeded right to the point "—you're not a logger."

His eye widened in surprise.

"Who told you that?"

"Adam."

"He did?" Now Toeless's good eye shifted sideways. "So how much, exactly, do you know?"

"Not much. But if there's something—" she discarded the word *illegal,* this time "—dangerous about this situation, I think I have a right to know, don't you?"

"Ms. Duncan—"

"Laura."

"Laura, listen. You seem like a nice person. My advice is to forget whatever you've heard. But rest assured, Adam Scott is not a bad man. In fact, he's a very good man. The most solid and kind and upright guy I've ever known. But he's been badly hurt—"

"I know. His wife and child were killed in the

accident. Does his being upset with you have anything to do with that?''

"Why would you think so?'' Toeless seemed guarded.

"Seems to me that it's only been a year, and it would still be the major problem in his life— losing them.''

Toeless sighed heavily. "It is. And I didn't help. He's still so raw, so guilty, about the accident.''

"Guilty? You mean survivor's guilt?''

"Oh, no. Adam's guilt goes way beyond survivor's guilt. He feels directly responsible for the accident.''

"Because he was driving?''

Toeless didn't answer. He stared off at the sinking sun, biting his lip as if considering, as if remembering something, but keeping what he remembered to himself. "They weren't even supposed to be with him. I shouldn't have mentioned Elizabeth and Anna...'' He fell into a dejected silence.

"You're his friend,'' Laura said. "I'm sure he realizes you didn't intend to upset him.'' She placed a gentle hand on his arm. "How long have you known Adam?'' she asked.

"Since junior high. He was the clean-cut kid, the town genius, class valedictorian and all that.

I was the kid whose hair hung in strings down the bridge of his nose—'' he pulled a strand forward to demonstrate ''—the bad boy, the first to get a motorcycle. I didn't like him and he didn't like me. I called him The Perfessor and he called me by my real name.'' He shot her a glance ''Don't ask. Anyway, about the third time that happened we got in a fight and he beat the crap outta me. Biggest surprise of my life. We've been buddies ever since.''

Laura smiled. ''That's so rare,'' she said sarcastically. ''A lifetime friendship...based on violence.''

Toeless smirked, then grew serious again. ''If you knew Adam... Believe me, lady, there's no finer man than Adam Sch—Scott.''

Laura frowned. ''Really? Down at my agency, he has a reputation for being difficult.''

Toeless snorted. ''Compared to the way he was six months ago, 'difficult' is a relief.'' He sighed again.

''The best way—the only way—you can help Adam is to fix his shoulder. That's your job. Get his shoulder back in shape. And don't worry, as far as danger goes, I won't let anything happen to you.''

Laura wanted to argue that she had the right to decide whether or not to put herself in danger.

She studied Elko's profile. He was a strange man, all right, but for some reason Laura found herself trusting him. Even though the eye patch, she suspected, was phony.

Toeless read her thoughts. "It's real. An injury when I was an ATF agent."

"You were an ATF agent, as in the Bureau of Alcohol, Tobacco and Firearms?"

Toeless nodded.

"A real tough guy, huh?" Laura smiled to hide her surprise. "I'm sorry. I thought it was part of your logger disguise. Why doesn't Katherine like you?"

"She thinks I'm a bad influence on Adam."

"A bad influence?"

"I'm only doing what he wants me to do."

"Which is?"

"You'll have to ask Adam. It's his story to tell."

"Well, can you at least tell me about Doc and Katherine's relationship to Adam?" Laura persisted. "I get the feeling they're more than just neighbors. Are they?"

His one eye fixed on her in a censuring squint. "You are a nosy little thing, aren't you?"

"You might be, too, in my place."

"Come on." Toeless stood, took her arm and pulled her to her feet. "I need to walk. Smells like Katherine's got something good baking down at the cabin.''

"Katherine said you chopped off your own toe," Laura said after they'd walked down the mountain a ways.

He stretched one boot forward, looking at the tip. "Katherine *would* put it that way. Like I was into self-mutilation or something. It happened a long time ago when I was a kid, chopping wood in my stocking feet.

"A snake slithered out of the woodpile and I panicked and hacked at it with the ax. Got my own toe, instead." He smiled and shrugged. "The snake went on his merry way and I went to the emergency room."

They were almost back on the path that led down to the main cabin when Toeless stopped and grabbed Laura's arm. With a finger to his lips, he signaled her to be quiet. He pointed at something to their right, back across the creek.

She looked where he was pointing and her mouth dropped open.

High up on a rock formation that jutted from the mountain, whuffing and rearing up on hind legs, was a bear. Two cubs frolicked among the shoulder-high willows down near the water, oblivious to their mother's watchful pose.

The sow's attention appeared riveted on Laura

and Toeless, and even with a rushing river between her and the bear, Laura's hair stood on
end. In all her backpacking adventures she had
never encountered a bear this close. Of course,
she and her friends always took precautions,
wearing loud bells, camping on established sites.

"A black bear," Laura confirmed quietly near
Toeless's ear.

"Yeah," he whispered. "They usually stick to
the brush along streams."

"So why is she down here?" Laura asked.

"There's a den below that cornice—could be
hers."

"What should we do?" Laura inched behind
Toeless.

"Stand still."

Laura had never stood so still.

When the bear finally dropped onto all fours
and lumbered off with her cubs hopping and
making baby-bear talk behind her, Laura and
Toeless drew deep breaths of relief.

"Do you know much about bears?" Toeless
asked in a low voice.

"Just that they scare me to death. Bears are
the one thing about the high country I'll never
get used to."

"Anybody ever explain the difference between a black bear and a grizzly?'' Toeless said as they continued up the path.

Laura nodded, but before she could explain the little she knew, he cut in. ''If a bear chases you up a tree, it's a black bear. If it knocks the tree down, it's a grizzly.''

''Very funny,'' Laura poked his shoulder. Toeless was a real character. But as they walked back down to the cabin and she studied his beefy back, Laura realized she liked him, trusted him. There was something very solid about him. Even when facing a mother bear, he was easygoing. So very unlike his lifelong friend, Adam Scott.

AT SUPPER, Laura and Toeless told Doc and Katherine about the bear.

''We'd better start wearing bells,'' Doc said. ''She could decide to come back.''

No one mentioned the fact that Adam had not put in an appearance at the table.

''Why didn't Adam come down for supper?'' Laura asked Katherine later, while they were washing the dishes.

''I don't know. I assumed you did.'' Katherine turned to her, surprised. ''What did he say during his afternoon treatment?''

''He missed the treatment.'' Laura finished drying the plate in her hands, then set it carefully on the chopping block. "Toeless said he got angry and went up on the mountain."

Katherine stood very still for an instant, then she relaxed and sighed. "Poor Adam."

"Yes. Poor Adam." Laura thought about the conversation she'd had with Toeless. She wondered if she could bring that up with Katherine. How much did this neighbor know?

There was pain, a terrible pain, that went even beyond Adam's obvious bereavement, hidden in this mess.

"Katherine, can I trust you?" Laura asked quietly.

Katherine turned from the dishes. "What do you mean?"

"I mean, something's not right. I overheard Adam and Toeless talking about Russians or something, really weird stuff. Something about a man named...Graddot?"

Katherine's parchment cheeks turned pink, then she faced the dishes, speaking with her back to Laura.

"Gradoff." She started scrubbing a pot furiously. "I told Adam he couldn't keep everything from you. But honestly, dear, all I can tell you is that I think you would be better off if you minded your own business."

"Everybody keeps saying that."

"Because it's true." Katherine's voice became firm, almost stern. "Adam has some things he needs to work out, that's all, but none of it involves you."

"It doesn't? What about when Adam came sneaking up into the attic while I was sleeping?"

Katherine dropped the pot in the dishwater and looked at Laura. "Adam would never do such a thing."

"He most certainly did do such a thing." Laura insisted. "He was using a pair of very high-tech binoculars. Night-vision ones, I think. As long as I'm staying here, in a way this *does* involve me. What's he looking for with those binoculars?"

Katherine turned and rinsed the pan carefully with scalding water from the big white kettle.

"Aren't you frightened by all this?" Laura demanded.

But Katherine didn't answer. With her mouth set in a tight line, she handed the rinsed pan to Laura, then crossed to the stove to put some cans of spice on a shelf above it.

Laura couldn't stand it. "Look, are we in danger or not?"

One by one, Katherine returned the spices to the shelf. Deliberately. Precisely.

When the job was done, she faced Laura again.

"There are things you don't understand, Laura. Things that might help you understand Adam and…your own situation here better. But I can't reveal them. All I can say is that, despite appearances, you and I and Doc are not in any danger, not on account of Adam." Then she excused herself in a whisper and left the room.

Laura stood there holding the pan and the dish towel, feeling more bewildered than ever.

ADAM DIDN'T SHOW UP for his evening treatment, either. No lights were visible in the stone house, and when they hadn't heard from him by bedtime, Doc and Toeless decided they'd better go out and search.

"I know the places where he usually goes," Doc said reassuringly.

No one spoke of the bear, but as Doc and Toeless tied the clanging warning bells to their belts, Laura began to feel a definite disquiet.

When the men were gone, she could not stop herself from asking Katherine questions again. "How much time has Adam spent up in these forests?"

"A lot." Katherine crossed the kitchen to peer out at the moonlit landscape. "Adam has spent hours and hours—days—in these woods. Hiking, canoeing, rock climbing. He's been to places you've probably never even heard of, sometimes camping in very rough terrain, in wild remote places, terrible places.''

Katherine turned and grasped Laura's arm. "We cannot be worrying ourselves sick about Adam. Adam is going to do what Adam is going to do. And he can take care of himself.'' She gave Laura a nod of finality and released her arm.

"If that's true,'' Laura responded quietly, "then why did Doc and Toeless go searching for him?''

"Because even the most experienced outdoorsman could have an accident.''

Chills broke out on her arms, and Laura rubbed them up and down. She suspected from Katherine's tone that the woman was talking about something even more ominous than bears. "Why has Adam spent so much time in the wilderness?''

"He...his work as a botanist takes him in search of exotic plants. Still, he shouldn't be alone in the dark.'' Katherine said this last more to herself than to Laura.

Again Laura wondered if there something even more dangerous than a bear out there.

ADAM LET THE RUSHING SOUND of the creek fill his head, hoping it would do its magic and drown out the names reverberating through him and the memories they evoked. If only Toeless hadn't spoken their names.

He'd worn himself out hiking, ending up in this spot, where he always did. Here, two flat boulders formed a narrow space and the river poured down in a ten-foot-high waterfall. This was a place where it was possible to forget. A place where the ceaseless noise and motion of the water cleansed him of his painful memories.

But not tonight.

If only Toeless hadn't spoken their names. In the first weeks after the accident he'd wanted to hear their names all day, every day. He'd wanted people to talk about them as if they weren't gone. Wanted them to repeat the favorite anecdotes, note little things they would have liked, recall things they had said. It was as if he was keeping them alive somehow with the sound of their names.

He wouldn't let anyone touch any of their belongings. His mother and sister had come up from California three times to do the sorting and the packing. Three times he'd refused to allow it.

Finally, when his family seemed unable to cope with his grief, when they no longer had the strength to dwell on Elizabeth and Anna every single day in every single conversation, they'd left. He knew he'd driven them away. He hired a team of strangers to pack up the entire household, not just Elizabeth and Anna's things, but everything.

He'd shipped it all to the Joneses' house in Seattle, because he hoped that, unlike him, they would be able to stand the little reminders of Elizabeth and Anna. He had no idea what they'd done with the stuff; this had become one of many forbidden topics.

When he'd recovered from the accident enough to travel, he'd left the empty house to a Realtor, with instructions to sell below market value if necessary, to just get rid of it.

Then he'd come here. He drew in a deep breath of the misty mossy night air. The forest. He'd come to this mountain to heal. Only he hadn't. And so he'd finally realized he had to do this other thing. He drew a deeper breath, felt stronger, clearer, just thinking about his plan.

He blinked. The moonlight reflecting off the waterfall created a kind of screen, and suddenly he was reliving that night, the road twisting like a black snake in the darkness as he drove faster, faster.

"It's Gradoff!" Elizabeth cried as the Jeep

that had butted their rear bumper now pulled up between their minivan and the mountainside.

"I saw his face! He wants the damned formula!"

Adam turned to glance at her, but she was already in the back seat, frantically wedging pillows and a sleeping bag around Anna's car seat.

Elizabeth knew nothing about the laundered investment money, nothing about the key-man insurance, nothing about the very real danger they were in.

He managed to put distance between the Jeep and the van, rounded a sharp curve, felt the tires leave the pavement.

"Give the damned thing to him, Adam!" she yelled. "It's not worth it!" She grabbed the sides of the front seats and leaned forward, her eyes fixed on the road and wild with terror.

"It's not the formula they want," he began, then stopped. Now was not the time to tell her the truth: that he'd withdrawn from the deal and threatened to go to the authorities because he'd discovered the funding came from laundered black market money. Now was not the time to remind her that he was the key man, the irreplaceable scientist, and that he was suddenly worth more to them dead than alive.

She turned to look behind them. The Jeep's

headlights were still there. "Surely we'll come upon another car or something soon." She grabbed the cell phone. He heard the beeps as she punched 911.

Anna was crying, "Mommy!" and Elizabeth pressed as close as possible to the child, while she held the cell phone to her ear. He heard Elizabeth talking frantically to someone, but how far away was that help?

Adam glanced in the rearview mirror at the headlights of the Jeep closing in. He sped up, but the Jeep only gained ground.

His palms grew slick with sweat on the steering wheel as he rounded the next sharp curve.

The Jeep struck them hard and the minivan flew into a downhill skid. Adam fought the wheel like a mortal enemy, but the force was too powerful. He lost control. He felt one wild jolt, and then a strange second of weightlessness as the van went airborne over the side of the mountain.

He threw his right arm back, toward Elizabeth and Anna....

Adam shook his head, but was unable to stop the memories. He'd come to, feeling as if he was underwater. Black water. He'd shoved at the airbag and touched his fingers to his eyes, which felt sticky. Blood. He was conscious, even though he couldn't hear, couldn't see. But he could feel. Searing pain in his left side; his right arm and shoulder were numb.

And he could smell. Gasoline.

He had to get them out of here! He ordered himself not to panic, moved his legs, wiggled his toes. His loafers were gone.

"Elizabeth!" he called. "Elizabeth! Anna!" His own voice sounded muffled. Why wasn't Anna crying? He wiped the blood from his eyes. The headlights of the van pointed up at a crazy angle. He twisted in the seat as far as he could. The top of the van was smashed low. The big side door was gaping open. The rear window was broken out, completely missing.

So were Elizabeth and Anna.

He unhooked his seat belt, dragged himself up through the broken windshield and looked past the maze of black tree trunks, up the side of the mountain toward the road. A pair of headlights beamed into the darkness from the shoulder.

"Help!" Adam screamed. "Down here!"

But the headlights veered away, and he heard the squeal of tires on blacktop.

He scrambled out over the crushed front end of the van, charged around in mad staggering circles for a full ten seconds, crying their names before he thought to go back and dig around in the glove box for the flashlight.

The smell of gasoline was stronger. He worked quickly, panning the wreckage with the flashlight, but it was only when the van burst into flames that he had enough light to locate them.

Elizabeth lay facedown about twenty feet away. He pulled up her limp, lifeless body, hugged her to him and tried desperate, futile CPR. When it failed, he cried out to God.

Anna had been thrown farther. She was still strapped in the car seat. He seized the whole apparatus, clutching it on his lap. He clawed at the straps, rocked her, sobbed over her downy head until everything that could possibly pour from a man had run out.

Only later, when he was stumbling down the mountain road shivering with shock and choking on bile, did he feel the disk that he'd zipped into the pocket of his jacket. He stopped right in the middle of the road and shone the flashlight on the red plastic case. The formula.

And Elizabeth had sealed the prototypes in the secret compartment built into the back of the frame of her wild-iris print watercolor when the trouble had started.

By then he'd no longer cared. Maybe as early as that terrible night, he'd formed his plan to use himself as bait to destroy Gradoff and his men....

Now Adam stared at the waterfall. He rubbed his eyes. No tears. Never any tears.

He stood and took the few steps to the creek. He bent down on one knee and cupped a handful of the freezing water and splashed it into his aching eyes. Then he scooped another handful into his mouth and rinsed the familiar salty taste of remembrance away.

If only Toeless hadn't spoken their names.

IN LESS THAN AN HOUR Toeless and Doc returned to the cabin with Adam, and no one gave any explanation to Laura.

"Don't worry about the treatment," was all Adam had said before he stomped out the back door.

Alone in the attic room that night, Laura wondered again if she could ignore all these strange things and finish the next five weeks of therapy. And more worrisome, could she ignore her feelings of attraction to this man?

Much later, in the dead of the night, she heard the downstairs door to the attic creak open, then soft footfalls on the stairs. She turned her head so she could see, then lay perfectly still.

It was Adam. He stopped at the landing, gripping the rail. In the darkness she could make out his head as he turned, and she knew he was studying her.

Then he crept to the high window at the other end and stood there, looking out on the scene below with the binoculars. After a while he tip-toed away and stopped again at the top of the stairs to look at her.

The waxing moon etched his features, and Laura thought she saw a new sadness in his face. He tilted his head back and released a sigh into the darkness.

When he'd crept back down the stairs, Laura let her feelings surface. She was not only afraid, she was angry. She tossed back the covers and swung her feet over the side of the bed, knocking Ned over in the process.

She sat there considering her many options: calling Sylvia and telling her to get someone, even a practical nurse, up here to replace her immediately; confronting Adam Scott about his strange behavior; simply leaving this place without notice or explanation—or her salary.

How dare he steal in here during the night, even if Doc and Katherine were sleeping directly below them, and…and…*stare* at her. His behavior was totally unacceptable.

She reached down to straighten Ned, and as

she gazed at his ever smiling face, she knew what she was going to do. If Adam Scott thought he could get away with these nightly activities, he was sadly mistaken.

CHAPTER NINE

SHE DIDN'T HAVE to wait long for her plan to
work. Two nights. She heard the door at the bottom of the stairs creak open again, and she was
ready.

Earlier, after she'd gotten Ned into position
she'd given the dummy a little shake as she
straightened him. "You're a good actor, pard-
ner," she whispered to his painted face. "If he
shows up, give it your best."

The moon was full now and it shone directly
into the big window, illuminating the silent Ned,
who was casually "leaning" against the newel
post at the top of the stairs. Perfect.

As she heard the creaks of the steps, she eased
out of the bed and stood in the shadows. When
Adam made it to the top of the stairs, he yelped,
startled, and knocked the dummy over.

Ned's hat bounced off, landing near Laura's
feet. Adam stepped forward, bent down and
calmly picked up the hat. "Very funny," he said.
He held the hat out to her.

Laura kept her arms tightly crossed. "I thought it was," she said, but there wasn't a smidgen of humor in her voice.

"Okay, Ms. Duncan." Adam tossed the cowboy hat on a chair. "I get the message."

Laura stepped into the moonlight, fully dressed in sweats. "Do you? Do you really?" She took another step forward, coming almost nose to nose with him.

"Of course I do," Adam said, holding her gaze. "But you could have just said something. I honestly didn't think I'd disturb you."

"That's hardly the point. The fact is, this is my *bedroom*. What are you looking for with those things?"

"I told you, it doesn't concern you."

"Oh, right. I forgot. My duty is to get your shoulder in tiptop shape. Well, how am I supposed to do that, Mr. Scott, if you won't show up for your treatments because you're too busy moping around the woods feeling sorry for yourself?"

Laura regretted the words as soon as they were out of her mouth.

Adam said nothing. He merely stepped past her and walked to the window. He raised the binoculars and stood gazing out of the window.

When he finally lowered them and turned to her, she saw anger in his eyes.

"Is that what you think I'm about?" he asked coldly. "Self-pity?"

Laura looked away, but he grabbed her arm and spun her around. "Sorry for *myself* is hardly what I feel, lady."

"What *do* you feel?"

He dropped her arm and looked at her with unmasked pain for one fleeting instant. "You wouldn't understand."

"Toeless told me you blame yourself for the accident," Laura said simply.

Adam squinted at her. "Toeless is sure loose-lipped for a PI. I guess I'll have to dock that guy's pay. Good night Ms. Duncan." He turned and descended the stairs.

CLIMBING THE PATH to the stone house, Adam thought about that stuffed cowboy standing sentry at the top of the stairs. And then he saw himself foolishly panicking and knocking the thing aside. He smirked. Poor old Ned. Then he smiled. Crazy woman. Then he started to laugh.

His laughter echoed off the tall pines. The sound of it made him laugh even more, as if he was some kind of madman, laughing alone out in the dark woods just for the hell of it. He laughed until the tears ran and he had to sit down on a rock to catch his breath. Crazy, crazy woman.

But later in the night, he awoke from a fitful sleep, thinking about her again, and this time there was nothing funny about his thoughts. He saw her standing in the moonlight, her pale fluffy hair translucent, her breasts lush.

Laura Duncan, of all people, had stirred something in him. Something he could have sworn he'd buried. He rolled onto his back and frowned. And then, despite everything, he found himself smiling again. Because this yearning felt so good. After all these long months it felt so very good.

He propped his hands behind his head and stared out the window at the moon.

Laura Duncan. His physical therapist. He wanted her.

"GOOD MORNING, dear," Katherine said pleasantly when Laura came downstairs the next morning. Laura had already looked out her bedroom window and seen Doc chopping away at the spent plantings in his garden. Higher up on the mountain, Toeless's tent, surrounded by morning mist, looked zipped tight.

"Where's Adam?" Laura said as she accepted the mug of tea Katherine offered.

"Well, I guess he's still up at the stone house. It's a bit early yet for his treatment, isn't it?"

I don't want to give him a treatment, Laura thought. *I want to talk to him.* "Mind if I take the mug up with me?" Laura lifted it as she headed for the door.

"Of course not. But be careful climbing," Katherine said. "The dew makes the stones slippery."

There couldn't have been a finer mountain morning. The sunlight shot up over the ridge of mountains. Everything glowed with the soft fading green of late summer. A hint of frost here and there made patches of the air seem caught in frigid stillness. Her breath came out in pleasing little white puffs. Too bad she and Adam Scott were about to have words.

Maybe she should tell him this time that she absolutely couldn't stay. That this whole thing had gotten completely out of hand.

There was no sign of Morton as she knocked on the door of the stone house.

For a long time there was no response, and Laura wondered if Adam had pulled another of his strange disappearing acts.

Suddenly the door jerked open and Adam

stood there in thermal pajama bottoms, unshaven, his chest bare, nipples puckering from the cold.

"Ms. Duncan?" he said sleepily, and ran a hand through his tousled hair. He squinted at the sun, barely peeking over the mountaintop. "Is it time for my treatment?"

"I'm not here to give you a treatment," she informed him calmly. "We need to talk."

"Now?" he said. His eyes looked as if he hadn't slept at all.

Laura hesitated. Her accommodating nature almost had her saying, *You go back to bed, and when you've had your rest we'll talk.* But instead, she said, "Yes. Now. This can't wait."

He cut a yawn short and frowned at her, but after a moment he stepped back and held the door open.

"Have a seat," he told her, and waved a hand toward the leather couch. He rubbed the other hand self-consciously over his bare chest, though he had been taking his shirt off in front of her several times a day. "Let me grab a shirt and some socks. It's, uh, chilly."

He rummaged in a pile of discarded clothes, pulling out a flannel shirt and some heavy woolen socks.

Laura pretended not to see the mess and studied the prints of wildflowers while he dressed. At night they'd been fuzzy framed images at the perimeter of a darkened room. And during morning treatments she had always been so focused on her task that she never looked around much. But now she noticed how beautifully matted and framed and arranged the prints were.

There must have been two dozen. Not only the Montana varieties she loved—bitterroot, glacier lily, butter-and-eggs—but also varieties from other locales. Some of the prints were quite unusual. An especially beautiful watercolor of a wild iris hung above the bed. The frame was peculiar—a thick rounded oval of bare seasoned wood, hand-painted with dainty wildflowers.

He began to lower himself into the armchair facing her, but stopped halfway. "Would you like some coffee?"

"I have tea." Laura held up the mug. She knew there was no electricity up here and wondered how he made coffee.

"I'll be right back." He disappeared into a room at the back of the house.

He came back just as she was reaching out to trace her finger along the curved frame on the wild iris.

"Don't touch that!" he shouted.

Laura jumped and pulled her hand back.

He seemed immediately embarrassed by his rudeness. "Uh, it's very old. Rosewood. Been in the family for a long time."

Whose family? Laura wondered.

"The coffee will take a minute." He ran a hand through his hair. "I percolate it on a camp stove."

Laura nodded, folded her arms across her chest and walked back to the couch. He sat in the armchair facing her.

They were silent for a moment, then they both spoke at once.

"If this is about last night—"

"I came about last night—"

He frowned and scratched his beard.

She frowned and stared into her mug.

"I want to apologize—"

"I'm sorry I acted—"

"Go ahead."

"No. You first."

Laura didn't know where to start. The inviting aroma of fresh-brewed coffee drifted out. "The coffee smells wonderful," she said. "I'll have some, after all."

"Sure." He disappeared to the back room again and came back carrying two white mugs with steam rolling out of the tops. "Do you take anything in it?"

Laura shook her head and he handed her the mug. She had the same funny feeling she had on the night of that first cordial dinner with Doc and Katherine, and wondered, of the two sides of this man she'd seen, which was the real Adam Scott?

She set the mug on the low table beside the couch and decided to get right to the point. "Mr. Scott, I apologize for accusing you of feeling sorry for yourself, but I was very upset about your coming into my room. I don't know why you did, but under the circumstances, I think I should leave."

He'd brought his mug to his lips and now he looked at her over it, his eyebrows raised.

"I don't want an explanation," Laura continued. "I came up here to give you my resignation. And this time I mean it."

He frowned and set the mug on the table beside hers. Then he sighed, braced his elbows on his knees and stared. "Ms. Duncan," he maintained his pose for another instant, then raised his head and looked her straight in the eye. "I apologize for coming into your room. I...I should have told you. You see..." He stopped. He shook his head, then got up and crossed to the window, where he looked out, seemingly deep in thought. "I really didn't think I'd disturb you. And as I told you before, I'm not taking any chances up here.'' He shot a glance at her. ''I guess I'm not making much sense. I...I don't know what to say, except I truly am sorry.''

''I believe you. But you're still not telling me why you're sneaking around in the middle of the night. I'd like to know what you're looking for.''

He shook his head again. ''I'm sorry, but I can't give you details. Please try to understand that I'm in a difficult position here. For reasons I can't explain to you, I can't leave this mountain right now. But I do need physical therapy on my shoulder—you know how badly. And since it's too far for someone to make the trip several times a day, and since I'm willing to pay an exorbitant sum...''

''Not enough to have my privacy invaded.''

''I understand. It was wrong of me. But the large window in the attic is the only vantage point where I can see the entrance to Sixteen Mile Creek Road. I have an electronic sensor down there. I've been checking whenever it's activated.''

''Why would you have something like that? I think I have a right to know.''

He steepled his fingers against his lips and studied her. ''All right,'' he finally said, ''I'm aware you've overheard some things...but you aren't in any danger, I promise you that.''

"I'm not?"

"No. As I said before, this...situation is a business problem, business intrigue, if you like. And it's absolutely none of your concern, Ms. Duncan. But I'll need your permission to come up to the attic to check the road from time to time—"

In case the Russians are coming? Laura thought dryly.

"—and I promise not to disturb you. I'll keep to the other end of the attic. Or perhaps we can work out some other way to make you more comfortable. Install a screen or a curtain. There must be a way..." He reached up and rubbed his shoulder.

Laura stood and paced the rug. Then she stopped and looked at him. From his place by the window, he watched her, with his hands loose at his sides as if he was waiting patiently for whatever would come. Despite the strands of silver in his hair and the crinkles at the corners of his eyes, something about his face seemed as innocent as a schoolboy's. Despite all the strange things she'd seen and heard, something about him—maybe his eyes—made her trust him.

Laura looked into those eyes. Possibly for the first time, she realized. And what she saw was the opposite of what she'd seen the first time she'd looked into Stuart's eyes.

Back then, she'd ignored what she'd seen: Stuart's duplicity, his selfishness, his arrogance. Was she going to make that mistake again? Was she going to stand here and ignore what her heart saw in this man's eyes? The sincerity, the kindness, the...she kept staring at him, as words like *intelligence* and *depth* drifted across her mind, until she ended with one simple word: *goodness.*

"I just want to be safe," she said softly.

"Of course," he answered, and took a step toward her. "You have that right. And I promise that you are. Please stay."

"Okay," she answered.

He smiled. "Thank you, Ms. Duncan."

"Please call me Laura."

He hesitated, holding her gaze for a long moment. "All right, Laura. Thank you."

She told herself that she'd agreed to stay because of her softheartedness, because of her professional integrity, because of a lot of reasons except, she finally admitted to herself as she lay awake that night wondering if he would come up the stairs, the real one—that she was attracted to him.

AFTER BREAKFAST, during his therapy, Adam asked Laura's permission to work up in the attic for a couple of hours. He and Toeless hauled some lumber and tools from the shed up the stairs. Doc insisted on making the painful climb up the stairs and then the sounds of construction started.

A steady din of sawing and hammering still echoed from above while Katherine and Laura fixed lunch.

"What on earth are they doing?" Katherine asked, rolling her eyes toward the ceiling.

"Building some kind of wall, I expect," Laura said with a sigh.

At Katherine's puzzled look she added, "It's a long story."

When lunch was ready, Laura and Katherine took the men some cheese sandwiches so Doc wouldn't have to come down the stairs. He was sweeping up sawdust. Adam and Toeless were on their knees, stapling white fabric to a rough six-foot frame built with two-by-fours down the center of the room.

"My unbleached muslin!" Katherine exclaimed. "That's for quilting!"

"You'll never use all that stuff." Doc waved a hand dismissively.

"I'll get you some more." Adam soothed Katherine as he stood. "I wanted to surprise

Laura.'' He looked in her eyes and walked toward her.

''We did it this way—'' he took hold of her arm and guided her around the barrier ''—so the light from the big window would still filter into the bed area.''

The moment he touched her, Laura caught her breath. She'd been trying to deny the magnetism she felt when she touched him, but she couldn't deny this. When *he* touched *her,* it was ten times worse. His warm fingers held her arm gently but firmly, and she could feel the restrained power in his hands. Suddenly she felt a wave of physical desire.

When they stepped around the cloth screen to where the bed was, the room, softly lit by the filtered noonday sun, seemed altered, transformed. Intimate.

''See?'' he looked at her, and she held his gaze. The look they exchanged said everything. It said, *We're alone behind this screen and I'm touching you, and I'm not letting you go. I want you, and you know it and I know it, and now what?* It said, *You're touching me, and I can hardly breathe and why now? Why am I falling in love with a man who's been through all that you have? Why you?*

Adam's grip tightened on her arm. He pulled her a degree closer. "Laura—"

"Yes, I see," she said quickly, softly. So softly she was afraid he might guess what she was feeling. "It's...it's nice."

They stood there for that endless moment, breathing and staring into each other's eyes while he held her arm and she didn't pull away.

"Hey—" Toeless poked his head around "—aren't you two gonna eat?"

Instantly Adam let go of Laura's arm, but Toeless's eyebrow shot up over the eyepatch before he looked away. "You guys hungry?" he said as if he'd seen nothing.

"Starving," Adam murmured.

IN THE DAYS FOLLOWING, Adam began to talk to Laura during the treatments. Only about small unimportant things, but it was obvious he was trying to make her more comfortable. And he even started making jokes.

One evening when she was looking through her CDs for the perfect workout music, Laura pumped her eyebrows and whipped out a CD. "Perfect! Carly Simon's 'Coming Around Again/Itsy-Bitsy Spider.'"

Adam rolled his eyes as she put the disk in

the player. He listlessly started his reps on the
finger ladder.

As the beat of the song picked up, Laura
started humming, then in a twangy accent, she
sang along. Adam looked solemn as he recognized the lyrics but Laura didn't give him time
to brood. She pulled him up off the couch,
plunked his good arm over her shoulder and
twirled him around.

He started to object, but before he could say
anything, she pulled him sideways, leading as
she danced him lightly around the small room.

Adam resisted. "Laura, what *are* you doing?"

"You're getting bored with the reps—" Laura
gave him a shake "—so we're gonna dance!"

"I do not dance," he said seriously.

"Listen. I'm the boss here and I say it's time
to dance!" Laura swung him around in a tight
little spin.

She told herself this was therapeutic, if not exactly traditional therapy, and while they danced
she could carefully manipulate his arm up, down
and out, creating excellent extension and flexion.
And, she reasoned, dancing was therapy for the
spirit. And in Laura's opinion, this man sorely
needed that.

But who was she kidding? Laura knew she
was testing, too. Testing to see if that touch that

had sent her into such a tailspin only a few days before had been real. Right now her pulse was racing and her breath was coming faster—that part was real—and she was glad the silly dancing covered her response.

And Adam? Was he for real? He certainly *felt* real. And he certainly looked real. His mouth, his firm lovely mouth, was only inches from hers. She'd never seen a more appealing man. But what was he really like, Adam Scott, when he wasn't having thoughts of grief or vengeance? More than anything, that was what she wanted— to know the real Adam Scott. The solid and kind and upright guy Toeless had talked about.

Adam danced stiffly at first, with a wide-eyed disbelieving expression on his face that made Laura smile.

Laura sang breathlessly as she jigged about, crooning more loudly as both the song and their dancing picked up steam.

Adam was still looking at her as if she was demented, but at some point he stopped resisting her movements. His cheeks, she noticed, were starting to get flushed and she saw the hint of a grin. *Good.*

Adam watched this outrageous woman in his arms and thought he was like the spider, climbing back up. Did he want to feel this way again?

he wondered. Could he allow himself that and still do what he had to do?

But just like the night she'd slipped on the cherries, he couldn't help noticing the little details of her person—how her eyes turned into merry little slits when she laughed, how deep her dimples were. And now he noticed, also, how very tiny she felt, how intoxicatingly good she smelled.

Laura tossed her hair and a curl got caught on the frame of her eyelashes, but she ignored it, singing blissfully, her Texas accent twanging.

Adam had to smile.

When the song ended, they stopped, breathing hard, still holding each other, looking into each other's eyes.

Belatedly Adam loosened his arm from her waist and released her hand.

"Was that supposed to be therapeutic?" he said, embarrassed that he'd held her a second too long.

"Well, you tell me. How does your shoulder feel?" Laura pushed her hair back.

"My shoulder?" He grimaced. "Ooohhh!" He howled as he doubled over in fake pain. "Oh, God! My shoulder!"

Laura would have cheerfully slapped that

shoulder if she hadn't been trying so hard to heal it.

BUT NO MATTER how Laura succeeded in bringing him out of his shell during the treatments, between times Adam continued to disappear into the woods like a grumpy bear.

Laura felt she had too much time on her hands and started to look for ways to be useful. She made Doc some knee packs by filling a pair of tube socks with uncooked rice. She showed Katherine how to get the packs just warm enough in a skillet, then wrap the socks around Doc's knees at bedtime. The rice, she explained, would hold gentle warmth against his aching joints until he fell asleep.

She did whatever she could to help with the daily chores, and she and Katherine discovered their mutual love of cooking.

Then one day her restless eye fell on Morton. "How long since that dog's had a bath?" she asked Katherine.

"Oh, Morton won't let anybody bathe him except— He won't let anybody bathe him. Fights like a tiger, dear."

But Laura tricked Morton with a nibble of cheese, and with Toeless's help, gave the indignant dog a bath.

Because there was so little to do in the evenings, their suppers became pleasantly ritualistic: a bit of wine, Katherine's vegetarian cuisine and long conversations around the old oak table.

Doc and Katherine were artful conversationalists, and Toeless Elko turned out to be a talker of the first order. A fact that pleased Laura and seemed to irritate Adam.

Laura was relieved to have the attention drawn away from herself. She wondered if any of the others noticed how often her gaze strayed to Adam's face during these meals. The unanswered questions about this man tormented her.

Another week passed and they were at Katherine's house, taking a break from rolling out pasta for spinach ravioli, when Laura saw an opportunity to learn more about Adam's background.

"Were you ever married, dear?" Katherine asked her.

"Oh, yeah. I was married once." Laura wiped her hands on one of Katherine's hand-embroidered dish towels, then sat down at the table and started chopping spinach for the filling. "It wasn't a good marriage. With Stuart, it was more like a…business transaction."

Katherine frowned. "That doesn't seem like you to get involved in a loveless marriage."

"It's not like me. I've changed a lot since those days."

"Well, you're awfully good for Adam," Katherine said lightly as she filled the kettle with water. "He seems so much healthier, so much happier, since you've been here."

Laura always liked to hear that she was succeeding with her patients. "I hope I've been helping him. I can't imagine losing a family the way he did."

"No. No one can imagine that." Katherine turned off the spigot.

"Would you tell me about them—about his wife and daughter?"

Katherine turned to the counter. "Adam asked me not to speak of them."

"He *commanded* me not to." Laura shrugged. "I just thought it would help me understand him better. But it's okay if you feel you can't." She smiled and resumed chopping the spinach.

Katherine put the kettle on the stove to heat, then clattered around among the utensils in a drawer until she produced a small strainer. She took a teapot out of the cabinet, then a tin of herbal tea. She carefully loaded the strainer, screwed the lid on, then turned to Laura and opened her mouth to speak. But she stood frozen, with the strainer clutched to her flat bosom. Finally she forced out the words: "Would you like to see a picture?"

"A picture?" Laura said absently, then, "You mean of Adam's wife and child?"

This time Katherine didn't hesitate. "A picture of my daughter and granddaughter."

CHAPTER TEN

FOR A MOMENT there was a terrible silence.
Though she'd suspected the truth since that day
in the garden with Doc, Laura was jolted by
Katherine's words. She stood up, went to the
older woman and put her hand on her shoulder.

"Would you like to see their picture?" Katherine repeated softly.

"Of course I would."

Katherine went into the bedroom. In a moment
she returned with an antique brass oval frame
that held a professional-looking portrait done in
rich sepia.

"Oh, Katherine, " Laura said, running her fingers gently over the glass. "They're beautiful!"

Katherine smiled.

The fair-haired woman smiling from the picture looked familiar. Laura supposed it was her
strong resemblance to Katherine. She was slender, like Katherine, and had the same deep-set
eyes, high cheekbones and full lips. The little girl
in the picture was a miniature of the woman, ex-

cept she had Adam's dark eyes and dark wavy hair. The heads of the two were touching, and in the sepia tones, the contrast in their coloring was striking.

"Elizabeth was brilliant," Katherine said in a dreamy voice, "and Anna was so like her. She started talking before she was six months old. She called Adam 'Daddum.' From hearing Elizabeth say 'Adam' so often I imagine."

"Why doesn't he want you to talk about them?"

"He's afraid."

"Of what?"

Katherine sighed. "That we'll be discovered before he's ready."

Laura tried not to appear as frightened as that word *discovered* made her feel, but it was hard to be calm with her heart beating like a rabbit's. "Before he's ready?"

Katherine frowned. "I've said too much already. I shouldn't have shown you this, perhaps, but I knew you suspected the truth. I've been selfish, sharing this picture with you. Now you will have to pretend you don't know."

"I wanted to hear about them, and I want to know what Adam is getting ready to do. Please. Tell me," Laura urged.

When Katherine didn't answer immediately, Laura repeated, "Katherine, please."

The older woman sighed. "I wish Doc were here to help me, but these things have their own timing, don't they?"

Laura waited.

Katherine sighed again. "All right. If it will help you to understand Adam. The accident that killed Elizabeth and Anna and injured Adam wasn't an accident."

Laura nodded. She knew this much.

"The authorities… Adam reported it as soon as he made it down that terrible mountain road— before he even sought medical help for himself…" Katherine covered her mouth as tears came to her eyes.

When she recovered her composure, she stood to get the teakettle. "But, of course, the men responsible were long gone," she said as she filled two teacups.

"The men responsible?"

"Three men in a Jeep ran the family van off the mountain."

Now Laura covered her mouth. Hearing Katherine say it… "Why would anyone do such a horrible thing?" she mumbled through her fingers.

"They wanted…something Adam had."

"They?" Laura said, then answered her own query softly, "The Russians."

"Yes. How did you know that?"

"I heard Adam and Toeless talking."

"Oh, yes. My poor old mind is going quickly, I'm afraid."

"Who are these Russians?"

"Evil men. Backed by former KGB agents who are now involved in the international black market. They invested their laundered money in a...product Adam invented."

"Former KGB agents?" Gooseflesh stood out on Laura's arms. This was so bizarre. What had she gotten herself into? "What kind of idea?"

"Adam developed a plant compound—a pharmaceutical—microscopic oil droplets that protect people from germs and viruses." She sipped her tea thoughtfully. "They call them nano-explosives. A wonderful invention. But when Adam discovered that the money funding the project was laundered, he wanted to withdraw the idea from the investors. But they wouldn't allow it. You see, Adam is what they call a key man. In the academic world of biotechnology he is well-known—as Adam Schneider, that is. He has been using an alias since he went into hiding. The nano-explosive project cannot go forward without his expertise. The investors placed a huge life-insurance policy on Adam. Key-man insurance, they call it.''

Katherine stopped to sip her tea again, but Laura wasn't interested in hers. She was completely caught up in the story.

"Did Doc work on the oil droplets with Adam?'' She asked.

"No. Doc isn't interested in biotechnology. He's strictly a botanist of the old school. We bought this house years ago because Doc wanted to retire up here and grow things in this fertile soil. That's how Elizabeth met Adam. That forty acres up on the mountain has been in Adam's family since the Great Depression.''

Laura couldn't believe it. "*This* is where they fell in love?''

"Yes.'' Katherine smiled. "They loved it here. They built the stone house together. I'm surprised Adam moved back up there.'' Her smile faded. "He swore he'd never set foot in it again. This is where the story gets very sad, Laura.''

Gets sad? Laura didn't know if she could take much more of this.

"We were so happy when Elizabeth decided to marry Adam, a kind and good and brilliant man like her father.'' Katherine frowned and traced her finger along the gilt frame on the pho-

tograph of Elizabeth and Anna. ''I think it was
the arrival of the baby that made Adam want to
market his discovery. He wanted to make his
own fortune. Or perhaps it was just the excite-
ment and challenge of such a huge project, the
prospect of seeing his amazing breakthrough
used for the benefit of mankind.''

''Wow,'' Laura said softly.

Katherine stared at the picture. ''But now it's
as if Adam is being destroyed by guilt. You see,
he feels responsible for Anna and Elizabeth's
deaths, and he is using his prototypes—''

''Prototypes?''

''Models, samples if you will, of the droplets.
Adam hid them somewhere. He won't even tell
me or Doc where. He also has the only remaining
copy of the formula used to build the molecules.
He is using these things—and himself—to lure
the Russians here.''

''Why would they come here?''

''They want to kill him and make it look like
an accident. That way they can collect the key-
man insurance and recover the money. They'd
also like to get their hands on the prototypes, too,
I'm sure. A discovery like Adam's is worth a lot
of money.'' Katherine sipped her tea.

Laura stared at Katherine, considering all this.
How could the old woman be so calm about

something so frightening and dangerous? A sudden thought made Laura's jaw tighten. "I asked Adam point-blank if I was in any danger, and he said no. How could he stand there and tell me that, knowing all this?"

"That's where Toeless comes in." Katherine gave Laura a rueful smile. "He's not what he appears to be."

"Do tell." Laura hated her sarcasm, but all of this…conspiring rubbed her the wrong way.

Katherine apparently hated it, too. She echoed Laura's sarcasm. "Our darling Mr. Elko is a former ATF agent, lives on intrigue, but he's very skilled at protecting people. He works solely for Adam now. Even though I don't care for him, Adam trusts him implicitly. Gradoff and his minions don't make a move that Toeless doesn't know about."

"What about Adam's family? Don't they worry about all this?"

"They don't know anything about the laundered money, the key-man insurance or Adam's plan. They view Elizabeth and Anna's deaths as a horrible accident. They believe Adam has secluded himself up here to heal from his grief."

"I see," Laura said sadly.

The two women sipped their tea in contemplative silence, then Laura picked up the picture again. "You must miss them terribly."

"I do, but one can't look at the past for too long at a time. It's not good for the heart. This is what we are trying to help Adam see."

Katherine gently withdrew the picture from Laura's hands and laid it aside on the table. She looked into Laura's eyes, her own sad and serious. "And that is, perhaps, the thing you can help him to see—that he has got to stop looking back."

"I don't know what I can do."

Katherine gave her a wise little smile. "Adam likes you. I've seen the way he looks at you during dinner."

Laura blushed.

"He seems to be able to relax around you, Laura. Maybe you could take some opportunities, during the therapy, to remind him that life is for the living. You do like Adam, don't you?"

If Katherine only knew how very much Laura liked Adam. She wondered at times if she was falling in love with him. She nodded.

"I thought so." Katherine sounded satisfied. "That's why I took a chance and told you everything. I figured, maybe if you understood the seriousness of it all, you could help us turn him away from this vengeance."

Laura nodded again. It was true that she now understood Adam in a whole new way. She glanced at the faces in the picture and smiled. What she hadn't noticed before was the large golden dog standing behind the little girl.

"Was Morton Elizabeth's dog?"

It was Katherine's turn to smile again. "He was a stray she picked up down by the highway. Morton, I'm afraid—" she sighed deeply "—is a little like Adam. Spending too much time out in that woods…looking for her."

Laura closed her eyes.

"Thank you for telling me about them, Katherine."

"Laura, Laura, Laura." Katherine took Laura's hand and squeezed back. "You will be good for Adam. I sensed that from the moment I met you."

LAURA PONDERED Katherine's terrible story in her heart while the days rolled by. Adam's arm was growing stronger—and so were Laura's feelings for her patient.

Now every time she gave him a treatment, she stared at his muscular back and thought of Katherine's story, tried to think how to help him.

With her spirit so troubled, Laura found that the thing she missed most about Kalispell was

her church. She missed Reverend Green's silly
jokes; she missed the singing; she missed her
dear friends. But early in her stay here on the
mountain, she'd made a wonderful discovery: the
woods made a glorious chapel.

She especially liked to go back to the spot
where the rock cornice jutted out over the creek.
The forest stood older there, undisturbed, and the
sound of the waterfall was soothing.

She was sitting cross-legged on the rock in
quiet contemplation the following Sunday morning when Adam suddenly appeared on the high
boulders on the opposite bank.

She thought of that day when he'd come upon
her in this spot, how he'd scowled down at her,
how he'd seemed so unapproachable. How he'd
seemed, in fact, to resent her presence.

She pushed a lock of hair behind her ear as
she stared up at him, wondering what he was
thinking now.

He squatted down, balanced on the balls of his
feet. Something hung loosely from his hands. A
wildflower?

A smile seemed to form about his eyes as he
studied her quietly.

"What are you doing, Laura?" His voice carried clearly across the rushing water.

She looked down at her hands, folded in her

lap. "Since it's not practical for me to go to church in Kalispell, I'm holding my own service here." She smiled.

He looked down at the wildflower, rolled it between his thumbs.

"Church, huh?"

"Yeah. Want to come?" She spread her arms in invitation.

He smiled and shook his head, but he climbed down off the boulders nonetheless.

Laura felt happy anticipation building as he stepped across the natural bridge, then climbed the bank toward her. Maybe this was her chance to help him a little, as Katherine had said.

He moved up beside the cornice, and when he started to push himself up with his arms, Laura opened her mouth to warn him not to put stress on his shoulder. But before she could, he'd heaved himself up onto the ledge in one swift move.

"My, you are getting better!" she said.

"Thanks to you." He smiled as he made himself comfortable.

Laura felt herself blushing, but she didn't think Adam noticed. He'd crossed his long legs out in front of him and leaned back on his arms—both of them—with his face tilted toward the sun.

"So. I'm disrupting church." He squinted around at the wide-open spaces.

"Maybe it sounds silly to you, but this is a great place for it," she said simply.

He nodded and rolled the wildflower between thumb and finger, seeming to study it as the sounds of the gurgling creek and rushing waterfall made music. "Actually I can appreciate that. When I come out here, I get a feeling of…peace. Sometimes it's the only peace I feel for days at a time."

Laura's heart contracted. She wished she could give him instant peace. And joy and happiness and a whole lot of other things, including perhaps…love.

Abruptly he looked into her eyes. Laura swallowed as she returned his gaze. He had the most piercing eyes. And now that she better understood the dark pain in their depths…

The air around them suddenly seemed delicate, vibrating. A tiny moth fluttered nearby.

"Why are you looking at me like that?" he asked.

"I was just wishing this was all over for you—this healing—and that you were happy and fulfilled again."

To her surprise he chuckled. "Again? How do you know I was happy and fulfilled before?

Maybe I was a sorry, ill-tempered bastard who made his wife miserable and his child insecure.''

"I wouldn't believe that if the pope himself told me so,'' she said with conviction.

"Why not?''

"Because I am a very good judge of character.''

He raised a skeptical eyebrow. "What about your husband? Were you a very good judge of character when you married him?''

"Actually, being married to Stuart is what made me a good judge of character.''

Adam gave her a wry grin. "Yeah, I can see how that could happen.''

She shrugged. He probably knew more about Stuart, through Toeless, than she did.

"What were you thinking about when I saw you?'' he asked. "That is, if it's any of my business.''

Laura was glad he'd changed the subject, although the answer to his question was, of course, him. She wasn't about to tell him that, though. "I was thinking about lots of things. Mostly about how great it feels to be alive.''

Adam gave her another skeptical glance. "I wish I shared your sentiments.''

"It's not sentimental. Appreciating life is part of my faith.''

He frowned. "I suppose you believe in heaven and the whole bit."

"I believe there is a heaven, although I won't know what it's like until I get there," she answered carefully.

"That must be very comforting." He flung the wildflower into the water with his bad arm, then rubbed at his stiff shoulder as he stared off into space.

Laura spoke her next words softly, gently. "I also believe that love, which comes from God, can heal anything."

He turned to her, and his face mirrored the battle within him so clearly it almost broke her heart. "Once again," he said quietly. "I wish I shared your sentiments."

"Once again," she replied softly, "It's not sentimental. It's what I really believe." She reached up then and touched his cheek with her fingertips, looking into those sad eyes. It seemed only natural to touch him. She'd been touching him with care for weeks.

He grasped her hand and pulled it away, but only an inch. He closed his eyes and squeezed her fingers. "Laura," he whispered, "don't get involved with me."

To LAURA'S SORROW, the mood between them as she administered treatments became tense again.

She sensed Adam withdrawing into his own dark thoughts. Maybe he thought she was shallow, capable of offering only pat solutions to his problem. Maybe he thought she couldn't understand his pain. Oh, but she could. She *did*. How could she show him that?

Today he was especially quiet. A sweat broke out on his brow as he pushed his endurance on the arm bike.

Sitting near him on the leather couch, with the incongruous pulsing of the song "You Make Loving Fun" in the air, Laura wanted to laugh out loud at the irony in her life.

In fact, what she felt was a kind of hysteria, a kind of out-of-body craziness welling up as she sat there, biting her lip, watching his beautiful muscles flex.

How had she gotten herself into this bizarre situation? Living in a place so isolated that she had to travel seven miles down the road for a bath. Having to maintain a professional demeanor while touching this sexy compelling man every morning and every night. Enduring nightmares about Russian killers. And falling in love for the first time in her life. Here. Now. With him.

Even if she had tried to deny that last, she

couldn't deny the dreams that secretly used her hungering body to seduce her resisting mind. Dreams that clung to her like misty ghosts all the next day, whispering, *This is the one. There will never be another like him.*

He glanced at her, and Laura made an effort to compose her face. "Are you having any discomfort?"

He shook his head, but a moment later he winced and tilted it to one side.

Neck spasms. She had pushed him too far. "Stop," she said.

She went around behind the couch, stood behind him and massaged his neck. His skin felt hot and his muscles were as tight as steel cables.

Laura worked steadily. "Better?" she asked when she finally felt him relaxing.

"Thank you," he said so quietly that his words were almost swallowed by the music.

Laura's heart broke. She looked down at the top of his dark gleaming hair while he rotated his head from side to side. He never complained; he never gave up. So why did she feel so impatient, so angry with him?

"Let's go to the table," she said.

The sessions involved a lot more positioning now, a lot more aggression. Laura had to move him onto his side at times. They had to work together more and more, as a team. Constantly she circled the table, in front of him, behind him, reaching across him. Therapy had become like a familiar dance.

And just like the time they'd danced their real dance, their eyes occasionally met.

During the stretching maneuvers for the joint capsule, Laura again thought she read discomfort in his eyes. "Are we pushing this too far?" she asked.

He squinted as if weighing his answer. And suddenly her question had a double meaning. They both looked away.

Laura lowered his arm and gently pressed his shoulder back toward the table. "Roll onto your back and rest."

Adam rolled sideways, drew a huge breath, released it and looked out the window.

"Is something else wrong?" Laura asked.

"No." He threw his good arm up over his eyes.

But something *was* wrong. Below the arm that covered his eyes, the corners of his mouth were drawn down in what appeared to be a quelling of emotion, telling her more than words ever could. And though her heart ached for him, at the same time she felt as if she was losing her mind.

She glanced down the length of him to make sure he was safely situated on the high narrow table. But as he raised one knee, his foot slipped off the edge. Instinctively Laura reached across and caught the leg, with her breasts pressed into the thigh of his other leg.

He thrust himself up on his elbows, frowning. "Sorry," he mumbled as she straightened, then he emitted a sharp "Uh!" as the muscles in his shoulder and neck tightened from the sudden thrust up.

He lay back and groaned, his eyes closed.

"We have overdone it a bit," Laura stated. She pushed her glasses up on her nose and reached under his neck, massaging him expertly.

When he seemed relaxed again, she said, "I'm going to get the ice pack and make you a hot tea."

She turned and went into the back room to light the camp stove under the kettle.

ADAM WISHED TO HELL he'd never seen her sitting out on that rock. She'd looked so small and delicate. The sunlight had mixed with the color of her hair until the two were one. Now everything was really screwed up. Here, right in the middle of his scheme, arrives this woman with a heart, with a *soul*—the word brought him up short.

Yes. Laura Duncan had more soul, more…*joy* than anyone he'd ever met. She was, in fact, perfect.

Perfect body.

Perfect mind.

Perfect spirit.

Perfect touch. Somewhere in the past year, he'd forgotten about touch. The power of it. Laura was at ease with touching and, of course, that was the problem. She'd had to touch him from the start. When she'd brushed her fingertips across his cheek… When had he started to fall in love with her?

He thought of how irked he got every time Toeless brought her wildflowers, of how annoyed he felt at dinner when she and Toeless talked and joked and had a good old time. Annoyed, hell. He was just plain…jealous.

He suddenly felt as if one of the ancient trees outside had toppled over on him. Jealous.

And right on the heels of that realization came another one, just as startling. It felt good, great, in fact, to have these feelings.

He couldn't blame Toeless. She was irresistible. And hadn't Toeless asked him outright if he was attracted to her? And hadn't he said no? But he'd been lying. To Toeless and to himself. He was more than attracted to her. *He* should be the one bringing her wildflowers.

But he couldn't ask a woman like Laura, a woman with so much to offer, to get involved with someone like him—even if only physically, *especially* if only physically. Someone whose life revolved around plans of vengeance. Someone damaged.

He thought of how concerned she'd looked just now, glasses askew, when she'd caught his leg. Then immediately he thought of how soft she'd felt against him.

He had to do something about this, and soon, or he'd go crazy.

When Laura came back in, he drank his tea in silence while she made notes on her chart; she seemed ever mindful of achieving the goal. When she finished writing, she said, "Leave that ice pack on for another fifteen minutes or so," then she packed up her equipment bag, threw it in the corner and practically ran down the path to the big cabin. Did she feel it, too? he wondered. Could they get through the next two weeks pretending they didn't feel anything for each other?

THAT NIGHT, LAURA STOOD in the attic window looking at the glow of Toeless's flashlight panning the walls of his little orange tent.

Too bad she wasn't attracted to Toeless. He was the kind of big, lumbering, easygoing nice guy she *should* be attracted to. Instead, she'd fallen for Adam. Complex, challenging, dark-eyed, sexy, *grieving* Adam.

While she got ready for bed, she realized she'd left her record sheets on the table downstairs. As she moved along the hall she noticed a strange greenish glow coming from the main room.

She peeked around the corner and there was Adam, sitting shirtless at the oak table with the laptop screen illuminating his broad chest and strong features.

Doc's snoring droned softly from the alcove, there was no sign of wakefulness from either of the two older people.

Laura studied Adam's profile. He seemed deep in concentration. Suddenly his head snapped around and he stared at her, his eyes flashing darkly in the firelight.

Laura jumped as if she'd been caught spying on him. *Which is exactly what you were doing,* she chastised herself.

"Did you need something?" he demanded.

"I...uh...forgot my record sheets."

He looked across the table where the papers

lay in the shadows. The chair legs scraped, startling her. He snatched up the records and padded across the room to her on bare feet.

Laura hadn't put on her robe—she'd only intended to run down to the room for the papers and dash back up the stairs. She felt self-conscious standing there, also barefoot, in her gauzy cotton nightgown.

He held the papers out without speaking.

"Thank you," she said, taking them. "Well. Good night." She waited for him to return to his computer—she certainly didn't want to reveal her backside—but when he continued to look at her, she was forced to turn and exit down the short hall with as much dignity as she could muster.

"Laura." His voice stopped her at the kitchen door. "Could we talk for a minute?"

She turned to see that he'd stepped into the hall. His hands were braced on the door frame. His face was in shadow and his muscular physique was obliquely lit by the dim firelight in the room beyond.

"I guess," Laura's voice came out in a dry whisper.

"I don't want to wake them," he said quietly, and inclined his head subtly toward the little alcove where Doc and Katherine slept. "Let's go into the kitchen."

Without a word Laura walked into the small room. She went around to put the chopping block between them and turned to face him, but he wasn't there.

A moment later he appeared, carrying the cotton blanket Katherine had left out for his treatment that first day. "Here." He shook it out and draped it over her shoulders.

Laura's cheeks flamed. So he was as aware of the flimsy gown as she was.

"Here," he said again, and patted the seat of the stool.

Laura climbed up and hugged the blanket around herself. He leaned forward with his elbows propped on the butcher block and his hands clasped in front of him, the pose of someone about to address something difficult. "I need to tell you some things."

His head tipped forward and she couldn't see his eyes because he was looking down at his hands. But she heard him sigh. Evidently this wasn't going to be good.

"I'm sorry I haven't been an easier patient," he started quietly.

"You've been fine," Laura countered.

"Okay, then let's say I'm sorry I haven't been

a *nicer* patient.'' He glanced up at her, then cleared his throat when she didn't argue. ''And I'm afraid I haven't been completely honest with you.'' He pushed himself away from the chopping block and paced to the window where he stared out at the bright moon. ''In fact, I don't think I've been living all that honestly with myself since my wife and child died.''

He's going to talk about them? Laura waited, afraid to interrupt.

''I have to admit,'' he said, ''that I've allowed my grief, my moods, to rule my life. But just because my life is screwed up, that doesn't mean I have to ruin somebody else's. What I'm trying to say is, I feel badly because in many ways I've been unkind to you, and there's a reason for it, but it's not the reason you think.'' He paused.

When he spoke again his voice was throaty. ''Ms. Duncan—Laura—I think you should know that I am very attracted to you.''

Without giving her time to recover from the shock of hearing that admission, Adam continued, ''I think that's why I've been irritable with you, and that's wrong. It's unfair. You haven't done anything to deserve it. Nothing at all. In fact, you're...''

Words seemed to fail him and he paced away

from the window to a corner of the kitchen, near the refrigerator, farther away from her.

He leaned against the counter and ran both hands through his hair, pulling it tight against his scalp. Laura swallowed.

"What I'm trying to say is, maybe we shouldn't continue like this, up here, together. You may not be aware of the tension between us, but I am."

Was she going to be honest with him, too? Apparently not. Her throat was so tight she couldn't seem to speak.

"I know you must really need the fees from this job," he said quietly, "or you wouldn't have taken it in the first place. So don't worry about getting paid—I'll write you a check for the full twenty-five thousand first thing tomorrow. And don't worry about finding a replacement. I think I can continue the stretching maneuvers on my own now. I'm...I'm telling you that you're free to leave. And under the circumstances I think you should."

Why? Laura wanted to scream. *Why are you doing this now?* When I've become so familiar with you? So attached to you? So...in love with you? "You're sending me away because of your guilt," she argued. "Don't you see that?"

"You don't know what you're talking about."

How could she tell him that she *did* know without betraying Katherine? She had to think fast, to find a way.

"I heard you and Toeless talking," she blurted. "And I know you blame yourself for…for the accident."

He braced the heels of his hands against the countertop and hunched his shoulders forward, every muscle taut with emotion.

She came up beside him. "Don't do that," she said quietly.

He glanced sideways. "Don't do what?"

"Press against the counter that way. It puts stress on your shoulder capsule," she explained.

He shook his head. "You're amazing," he muttered. Then he cleared his throat. "You're a fine therapist and you've done a great job, but, Laura, I'm sending you away," he said, "and it's for your own good. You and I can't get involved with each other."

When he relaxed his arms and pushed away from the counter, Laura made a sudden move toward him, raising her fingers, parting her lips, meaning only to speak to him—she wanted to say something, anything, to reassure him—but her fingers touched his bare chest.

He grabbed her hand. "Don't," he said, and for a moment his face was a strange mixture of yearning and regret. Then his dark eyes ignited with desire. "Don't touch me," he whispered as he brought his mouth closer to hers.

"Why?" Laura whispered. She could hardly breathe.

"Because you deserve better." But with the last word he brushed her lips, and when their mouths met full on, it was as if they were mated already, right then, right there. Laura had never felt anything so real. She didn't know such warmth, such release, could be condensed into one passionate kiss. A kiss that had been held in check for weeks, for a lifetime maybe.

He pulled her tightly against his chest and his bare hot skin burned through her gown to fuse with her breasts. She could feel his heart pounding. She slid her palms up his back and felt a tremor pass through him. The kiss deepened and he groaned. His body responded to hers with such intensity there was no question in her mind about his wanting or her wanting or anything at all.

But just as she thought her heart might burst, he released her and stepped back. Breathing hard, she raised her hand and stepped toward him. "Adam," she said, but he grabbed her wrist and stopped her.

"No, Laura. If we get involved, if we let our-

selves feel things for each other... The last thing
I need from you is pity.''

Before Laura could answer, he turned and
moved swiftly down the short hall.

Laura folded her arms, closed her eyes and
lowered her head. "Oh, Adam,'' she whispered,
"the last thing I feel for you is pity."

UPSTAIRS, LAURA TOSSED around in Adam's
bed, fighting sleep...and her feeling for him. Finally, she jumped up and paced the floor until
she'd made up her mind.

Only once while making preparations, did
Laura allow herself a moment to wonder, *Is this
wrong?*

And for that fleeting instant she also wondered, even though she'd longed for this moment, dreamed about it, if part of her would regret going to Adam. No, she decided, it was far
more likely she would never forgive herself if
she didn't reach out to him. He was worth the
risk.

Laura finished dressing.

As she climbed the path to the stone house,
the night air closed around her, chilly and damp.
By morning there'd be frost, and the last of the
wildflowers would be damaged. This thought

gave her a sense of foreboding, and when Morton emerged from the trees, she dug her cold fingers into the dog's coat for warmth and reassurance.

But when they reached the clearing, Morton padded away into the dark woods, leaving her alone to face Adam. She looked up at the full moon, allowing herself one last chance to come to her senses before she raised her hand to knock on the door. But the beautiful moon only made her long for him more. She loved him. And if he didn't love her…well, he needed her. She was certain of that.

She knocked, and the door slid open on its creaky hinges, as if it had been left ajar.

"Adam?" she said quietly into the darkness beyond.

"Laura?" came his deep voice in answer, strangely alert, as if he had been waiting.

She pushed the door fully open and a shaft of moonlight wedged into the small room, casting her shadow on the floor.

He was in bed, propped up on one elbow, shirtless, with a wool blanket draped over him from the waist down. The curves of his muscled arms and chest flowed in statuesque relief in the light and shadow. Laura's breath caught in her throat, and she coughed softly.

"If we're going to be honest," she said when

she could finally speak, "I need to tell you something. I...I'm attracted to you, too. I thought you should know that," she finished in a whisper.

Was it joy or fear that caused his heart to pound so hard, Adam wondered. He couldn't decide.

He studied the vision before him. Her palm lay against the door seeming to steady her, as if she might fly away otherwise. The moonlight streamed through the unruly strands of her hair, and to him she looked like some sort of courageous angel, come to deliver him from his private hell. In some secret part of himself he'd wanted her to come to him, and here she was. Joy and fear.

She stepped inside and closed the door. When she spoke, her voice was tentative and low. "Adam? This is not about pity. Do you understand that?"

His heart pounded and he nodded. Then, realizing she probably couldn't see that in the darkness, he croaked out, "Yes."

She stepped into the pool of moonlight that poured through the window and stared directly at him for a moment. Then she turned her back to him, facing the moon. "It's not about pity," she repeated.

He swung his legs over the side of the bed. At

least he was wearing a pair of boxers. Heart pounding, he came up behind her. "Laura..."

She rested her palms on the sill and hung her head, no doubt listening, waiting for him to say the right words. But the words racing through his mind weren't the right ones, he felt sure. It was as if he were split in two. One part wanted Laura fiercely, wanted the warmth, the belonging, she held out to him. But the other part felt as if this move toward Laura was some kind of betrayal, some final act that would sever him from his family forever.

But he had to say something or she would leave. From the beginning, he admitted to himself, that had been his fear. He hadn't wanted her to leave. Was it because he'd seen her potential to give him this? This joy at the possibility of love...and this fear at the possibility of loss?

"Don't leave," he said, because that seemed to be all he could say that was clear and unconflicted.

"Do you mean, don't leave this place, or don't leave you here, now, tonight?"

"Both." Then he thought, *I mean, don't leave me—ever. Wait for me. Wait for my heart and my mind to be ready for you.* But he couldn't say it. Instead, he reached up and took a lock of her hair, holding it out in the moonlight, caressing it between thumb and forefinger. "Laura," he started again, "I'm not sure what I'm feeling, but it's so strong I..." He faltered because he wasn't sure what he could offer her, what he could promise her.

"Just tell me what you felt...when you kissed me." She kept her face toward the moon.

He squeezed the lock of hair in his fist, then dropped it. "Something I haven't felt in a long time," he said. *Something I thought I'd lost forever.*

She still did not look up at him. She took a huge breath and asked. "Was it something real?"

"Oh, yes."

She nodded, then removed her glasses and set them on the windowsill. Next, slowly, she peeled off her sweats. Underneath she wore a simple lace-trimmed cotton undershirt and matching tap pants. Her hair tumbled over her shoulders and down her back, floating out in filaments that looked like spun honey in the moonlight.

Adam's heart thundered.

"Laura, what are you doing?"

She didn't answer. She placed her hands flat against the top of her chest, closed her eyes and lightly slid her palms down over her breasts. She stopped with her palms crossed over her heart.

Adam swallowed. He couldn't remember ever seeing a movement so unabashedly feminine.

She released a great sigh. "What am I doing?" she finally whispered. "I guess I'm following my heart."

I hope I don't break that heart, Adam thought. He wanted nothing more than to lose himself in her soft fragrant femininity, but he didn't want to hurt her. How much of himself could he give to another? How much was left? He swallowed again and said, "Laura, are you absolutely sure about this?"

She turned slowly toward him and stepped forward, her bare thighs brushing his. "Yes," she said softly as she raised her mouth to his. "I have never been more sure of anything in my entire life."

She placed her fingertips on his cheek and pressed her lips to his. And for the first time since the night he'd thought his life had ended, tears stung in Adam Schneider's eyes.

CHAPTER ELEVEN

LAURA AWOKE to a pale dawn, chilled and alone in Adam's bed. But the pleasant aroma of coffee brewing from the back room told her Adam was somewhere near.

She pulled the covers tightly around herself and just lay there waiting, not knowing exactly what to expect now. After the incredible passion of the night the morning sun seemed like a censoring presence somehow, bringing common sense, bringing questions, to light.

After a while Adam came in carrying two steaming mugs of coffee. He was dressed— boots, jeans, flannel shirt.

"Good. You're awake. Here." He held out one of the mugs and smiled. "This will warm you up." She sat up in bed with the comforter pulled high around her nakedness and took the coffee from his hand.

Then to her disappointment he crossed the room and sat in one of the mission chairs, sipping his coffee and seeming to measure her with his gaze.

Was he sorry? she wondered. Disappointed? If he'd been thrilled with her, would he have jumped up and gotten dressed this morning? Did she compare poorly to… She blotted the thought out.

And was *she* sorry? No. She'd wanted this, she told herself. Had done it for the reason. Love. With no thought of what it might cost her.

"Do you want me to build a fire?" he said.

Laura shook her head and stared down into her mug.

"Can I get you anything else? Something to eat, maybe?"

Laura bit her lip. If he said one more courteous thing… To keep from crying, she fixed her eyes on the wild-iris print on the wall beside the bed. Adam, she reminded herself, was the one who had a right to cry. Not her.

She glanced at him. He'd been watching her as she studied the print.

"It's very old," he explained. "European. Has a small secret panel built into the back."

Laura pressed her eyes closed as she thought of Doc taking his little family to Europe, at the thought of his bright little girl who spoke many languages. Her heart hurt as she said, "It was hers, wasn't it?"

He kept his eyes on the print. "I can never forget them, Laura," he said.

"Oh, Adam," she replied softly, "no one would ever want you to. Making love to me doesn't mean you'll forget them."

He nodded, but to Laura something in his dark eyes seemed very unconvinced, very ambivalent. Watching him, all her old insecurities returned.

Had she done it again? Gotten herself involved with a man who couldn't, wouldn't, love her? But last night—last night he'd cried. He'd laughed some, too. And he'd told her he wanted her over and over. What had she expected? To erase his pain with one night of passion? She didn't know what she expected exactly, but it wasn't this...this *civility* between them. She couldn't stand it.

"I need to freshen up. I—"

"I warmed you a basin of water. I put out some soap and clean towels, too. Back there. I'll go outside so you can have your privacy."

Privacy? Laura thought. Wasn't it a little late for that?

"THE PUBLIC RADIO STATION said there's going to be a huge meteor shower tonight," Toeless announced jovially that evening as they all sat down to supper. "Anybody care to join me for a late-night viewing?"

He turned toward Laura expectantly, but she focused on her plate, sawing carefully at Katherine's tender eggplant parmesan as if it were a tough steak.

"My, that should be a sight!" Doc clapped his hands. "What time do you think it'll be best?"

"They said that the majority of sightings are expected between two and three a.m." Toeless smiled amiably at the older man.

"Laura, does the eggplant taste all right?" Katherine frowned at her. "You don't seem to have much of an appetite."

"No, it's delicious," was all Laura said.

Doc replied to Toeless, "Then that's when we'll need to be up on the mountaintop."

"We are too old to be getting up out of bed at all hours," Katherine snapped. "And walking up that trail? With your knees?"

"Laura—" she turned back to the younger woman "—are you ill? You don't look too good."

"My knees feel a hundred percent better since Laura's been treating them. You go ahead and get your beauty sleep, old woman. I'm watching the shooting stars while I've still got eyes to see with.''

"How about it, Adam?'' Toeless turned to his friend.

Adam said nothing, but Laura could feel him looking at her. She lifted her glass to take a sip of raspberry tea and made the mistake of looking over the edge into his eyes. The current that passed between them was almost painful.

"I'll go if Laura will,'' he said while he held her gaze. "How about it? Want to go look at the shooting stars with me and Doc and Toeless?''

There was a moment of silence around the small table. Laura looked at each expectant face. Doc's, Katherine's and Toeless's, all smiling. Adam's deadly serious. As if he'd asked her to donate a kidney or something.

''I like seeing shooting stars,'' she said hesitantly. "I...yes, I'll go.''

Adam nodded.

"Great.'' Toeless said. "No need to set your alarm clocks. I'll come around and get everybody up.''

Doc raised his wineglass high. "To shooting stars,'' he whooped.

Katherine flapped her hand at him, but Toeless raised his glass.

No one seemed to notice that Laura and Adam sat perfectly still.

"What nonsense," Katherine sputtered as the men sipped. "And with a mama bear recently about."

"We've got our bells," Doc said, and picked up his fork.

"Eat, then," Katherine said testily. "We'll need to get to bed early, if you're all bent on this foolishness."

The kitchen was clean and everything in order by eight o'clock. Toeless retired to his tent, Adam to the stone house and Laura to the attic.

After a while she heard Doc and Katherine's arguing voices rumbling up from below her—she supposed Katherine was still giving her husband a hard time about this "nonsense."

Laura had hardly slept at all when Adam, not Toeless, appeared at her bedside to wake her.

"Laura," he said, and for a moment she thought she'd drifted into another one of her dreams, "time to go look at the shooting stars."

She opened her eyes, pulled the blanket up to her chin when she saw his dark silhouette, then she sat up, her head clearing as she remembered the plan.

"Where's Toeless?" Her voice was scratchy from sleep.

Adam frowned. "He and Doc have gone ahead." Adam's expression softened as he studied her. "You sure you want to go?"

"Just give me a minute to get dressed." She glanced at the digital clock she'd brought with her from home. Two a.m. Exactly as Toeless had promised.

"I'll wait at the bottom of the stairs," Adam said. He walked around the muslin barrier and across the attic to the stairs.

Laura watched as he walked away. When he didn't look back, a vague disappointment settled on her again. A *real* lover would come and sit on the edge of her bed, touch her, or at least give her one last affectionate glance, wouldn't he?

She got out of bed and dressed warmly: hooded down parka over a T-shirt and sweatshirt—no point bothering with a bra—sweatpants over long underwear, two pairs of socks and her hiking boots. She pulled a stocking cap firmly over her curls.

"Katherine sure didn't like the idea of Doc getting up and coming out here in the middle of the night," Laura said, trying to make normal conversation as she climbed the path behind Adam. The sound of the bear bells made a jarring counterpoint to his silence.

"That's understandable," he replied.

"Of course. He's all she's got left in the world."

Adam stopped. She saw his back stiffen before he turned to her. "How do you know that?"

Laura realized her mistake and panicked. But then she reminded herself that they had a new bond now. Surely they could share things. "Katherine...uh, she told me. Adam, I know they're Elizabeth's parents. Please, don't be mad at her." Laura shook her head, causing the bell around her neck to clang sharply. "They love you, and they're worried about you."

He turned away. "God." Only that stricken utterance came through the darkness, but it sounded so bitter it set off an alarm in Laura.

"Adam, I..."

He didn't want to hear what she said. Instead, he began walking again, faster now, not waiting for her to catch up. "Adam, wait!" she called. "You have the flashlight!"

She could see well enough to make out his tall frame turning as the light flashed back in her direction, scoping down directly at her feet.

"I'm sorry." His bell clanged noisily and his boots skidded on the path as he came back her. "Here."

He took her hand and pulled her up the path to his side. When Laura felt the power of his muscles, she was reminded again of how much she loved this man. And how futile her love was. He wouldn't talk to her about his past. He didn't love her in return. When would she ever learn? As he pulled her steadily along, her unhappy feelings built until she couldn't bear his touch another second.

"Adam!" she cried, and jerked her hand.

"What?" He turned. "Was I hurting you?"

She carefully wriggled her hand free of his. "I'm fine. I…it's just that you don't need to hold my hand."

He stood there in front of her and slightly above, holding the beam toward the ground. But in the dim light she saw his chest rise and fall in a deep sigh.

Then his voice came out low. "Laura, I'm sorry. It's just that when you mentioned Katherine and Doc, I began to think about the pain I've caused them." He sighed again. "Laura, listen. I know they're worried about me, but you're not going to be able to fix all this by becoming my lover. The last thing I need is your pity."

"You keep saying that, but it's *not* pity. It's…" Laura couldn't bring herself to say the word *love*. Not yet. "It's caring."

"Pity, caring, call it what you like. You

shouldn't be getting emotionally involved with me.''

"Then maybe I shouldn't get *physically* involved, either, because I can't separate the two. Maybe what happened last night was a mistake." She balled her hands into tight fists inside her pockets as she waited for his reaction. When it didn't come, she glanced up at him.

His eyes glittered in the reflected light of the flashlight, but otherwise, his face was a shadowed mask. "All right," he said softly. "If you don't want me to, I won't touch you again."

He turned and resumed walking. "Stay close," he said, "so you can see the path."

Neither spoke as they continued up the remainder of the mountain. When they got to the clearing near the mountaintop, Laura saw that Toeless had built a campfire. Beside it, he and Doc had spread one of Katherine's old quilts. A bottle of wine and four tin cups lay on one corner.

"Welcome to my party!" Toeless greeted them.

Adam glanced at the cups. "No crystal?" he joked. But then he walked to the fire and stared moodily into the flames. Toeless and Doc seemed instantly uneasy.

"Would you look at that!" Doc exclaimed at

last, raising his arms to the star-filled sky. "It's like a sea of diamonds."

Adam gave the sky a glance, nodded thoughtfully, then walked over to a nearby boulder and sat.

"Aren't you going to sit on the quilt near the warmth?" Laura asked in dismay.

"The smoke gets to me," he answered.

Doc reached for Laura's arm. "Help me get down on the blanket," he said, diverting her. "Blast these old knees."

Toeless and Doc kept up their efforts to distract her, behaving as if Adam wasn't sitting several feet away on that rock, silent.

Toeless poured the cups of wine and the little group didn't have to wait long to see a shooting star. Over the next twenty minutes or so, they spotted at least a dozen, including one really long-lasting one that made them all ooh and aah. All, that is, except Adam, who remained as silent as the rock he sat on.

At last it was time to leave. Doc pushed himself up off the quilt stiffly, then tottered for a second while he pulled out his flashlight. Adam lurched off the boulder to lend Doc a steadying hand.

He gave Toeless some kind of silent signal, and Toeless jumped up beside Doc, too. "How

about if we head back down together, Doc?''
Toeless said. "I'm ready to get some shut-eye.
What about you, Laura?'' He turned and held out
a hand to her.

Laura let Toeless take her hand and pull her
to her feet. But as she bent to gather the quilt,
Adam said, "Laura…wait.''

She turned to face him.

"Would you stay up here with me for a minute?''

In the dark she couldn't see his face well, because Toeless had his flashlight pointed toward
Doc, who had set off on the rocky path down-
ward.

"Hold on there!'' Toeless called out.

Stubborn Doc merely waved a hand and kept
up his hobbling descent. Toeless hesitated.

"We'll catch up later,'' Adam said.

Laura stood where she was, clutching the quilt.

With a quick glance at Laura, Toeless hurried
past her. "Doc! You're gonna break your fool
neck!'' he shouted.

When the jangle of bear bells tied to Doc's
belt had faded completely, Adam asked Laura.
"Why did you get so upset when I took your
hand coming up the path? When I touched you.''

"I wasn't upset.''

He ignored the denial, took a step toward her,

raised her chin with one finger. "You can touch me, but I can't touch you. Is that it? You want to be the one in control?"

"No!" Laura twisted her face away. But maybe he was right. Maybe she felt okay touching Adam because he was the broken one and she was the strong one, the healer. "I just…I just don't want to get involved with someone who isn't interested in a serious relationship."

"Then why did you come to me last night?"

That was the big question, wasn't it? And she couldn't answer it.

He slid his hands into the pockets of his jeans. "There's something we've got to get straight before either of us touches the other again," he said. He looked directly into her eyes, his gaze narrowed as if he was issuing some kind of challenge, instead of talking about physical intimacy. "And that is, I can't…I can't be in love. Not with you or anyone else."

His words made Laura's chest ache and she turned from him, clutching the quilt more tightly. "How can you say such a thing?" she whispered.

He took her by the shoulders and turned her toward him. "I know it's impossible for a person like you to believe that could be true about anyone. But, Laura, you're too good for me to lead on. If anything more happens between us, you've got to understand what you're getting into.''

''I understand,'' Laura said softly, and looked away.

But Adam wondered if she did. He dropped his hands, and studied her smooth brow, the soft blond hair peeking out from under the stocking cap, the shadow below her full lower lip, the perfect swell of her breasts crushed together above the folded quilt. She was beautiful. So incredibly beautiful.

He should have let her go when she'd first wanted to leave the mountain. Hell, he should have *made* her go the moment he'd realized he was attracted to her, which, he admitted to himself now, was almost the moment he'd first seen her. Now it was too late. Now he couldn't let her go. He needed her. He needed her beauty, her life, her passion, her softness. Needed her warm heart, beating next to his frozen one.

He reached out a finger and tilted her chin up to look into her eyes. When he saw the tears forming there, something in him snapped.

''I want you so badly, Laura,'' he whispered, ''that I can't resist you.'' And with that he crushed her mouth with his.

At the contact she made a little strangled yearning sound, and that undid him further. Because it told him clearly that she wanted him as badly as he wanted her.

From somewhere a dim thought intruded—that to allow this intensity of feeling was somehow disloyal to Elizabeth and Anna—but he pushed that thought away because this wasn't even a question of allowing. This was something that demanded to be, this thing between himself and Laura Duncan. Right or wrong, this was what he wanted....

WHEN ADAM LET OUT an involuntary groan, Laura's heart sang. *Let him. Please let him feel everything a human being is supposed to feel at this moment. If only for this one night, let him have these feelings again.*

As he planted kisses in a path from her forehead to her chin, Laura told herself that she wanted only to give. But just as it had last night, the feel of his mouth sent a thrill through her unlike any she'd ever experienced, and she arched into him, suddenly greedy.

She filled her lungs with sweet cold air and threw her head back as he assailed her neck, kissing and tasting as if for the first time, for the last time, for the only time.

He stopped and let her go, leaving her reeling. He slipped the bell off her neck, then untied the one from his belt. He tossed them aside, then snapped up the quilt and shook it out near the fire. Suddenly he froze and turned to her. "What about birth control?" he said. "I worried about that this morning."

Laura forced herself to speak quickly. "I don't need it," she said as she fiddled nervously with the strings on her sweatshirt hood. "I'm…I can't get pregnant."

He looked her up and down, and Laura thought she saw a flicker of sadness in his eyes. Was he thinking of his lost child? He took two steps toward her, tenderly pushed a strand of hair out of her face. "Maybe that's just as well," he whispered.

Then he clasped her to his strong body again, and already Laura could feel the heat of anticipation pooling low in her center. He placed her on her back on the quilt, then pulled off the stocking cap and fanned her hair out with his fingers, making a flowing circle around her head. "You have such beautiful hair," he said, studying the halo he'd made. "Everything about you is so beautiful."

Laura swallowed, surprised at her immense joy in pleasing him. The truth was she loved him. Maybe she would be hurt, but she'd always have this night.

He touched her cheek. "And your skin—you have the most delicate skin I've ever seen. I'm afraid I'll irritate it—I haven't shaved. I'll be careful."

Laura shook her head, meaning, *No, don't be careful.* But still she couldn't speak.

He peeled off her jacket and worked the T-shirt and sweatshirt up. "I want to look at you again," he said as he did this. His voice, always low, was now husky. Hoarse. "I didn't get to look at you enough last night."

Again all she could do was swallow.

His breathing came more rapidly as he stripped off their tops.

Then he lay down beside her and slowly and patiently kissed her mouth and kept his warm chest pressed across hers, while he used his strong fingers and large palms to explore every inch of her exposed skin: throat, shoulders, abdomen, under her arms, over her breasts.

We should be getting chilled, out here in the cold, Laura thought when he pulled her onto her side, exposing her bare back.

Yet, in fact, the bite of the mountain air felt good, perfect against her hot skin. Everything—the worn quilt, the tart scent of the pine trees, the smoke from the dying fire, the starry sky—

felt perfect. Even their bodies had taken on a soft, surreal quality.

Laura watched in fascination as he knelt at her feet and removed her boots, then slid her sweatpants and thermals down over her hips.

"I've wanted you from the minute you stepped out of that stupid Toyota," he admitted, and when Laura nodded her understanding, he took his time looking at her body. In the starlit darkness she could see the unmasked desire smoldering in his eyes.

Adam's heart thundered as Laura looked up at him. Last night, he had believed that he wanted only to see, to taste, to touch her womanly form. But he had been surprised when instead of reacting merely to woman as he had intended to, he'd reacted to Laura. How could this miracle be? he wondered now as he felt it building again. But he wouldn't question it. His body was alive at last. Alive with her touch. Alive with wanting Laura, only Laura.

"Adam," she whispered, then closed her eyes and turned her head.

He took her in a move that was both demanding and surrendering. Or was she taking him? It was no longer clear. It no longer mattered.

He kept his mouth fastened on hers so that she couldn't even cry out when her great convulsion came, triggering his own as it did. Laura tasted his taste and breathed his breath and welcomed his essence into her, feeling a joy so great it was as if she were flying from the mountaintop to the stars and back....

When it was over, when they were both spent, when Adam's body relaxed over hers, he braced himself up on his elbows.

Laura immediately pushed at him to disengage them, trying to roll him over to his side. "Your shoulder!" she said. "You mustn't hold this position!"

"Don't," he murmured. "Don't push me away." He worked his palms under her buttocks and rolled them to their sides, pulling her more snugly against him, staying firmly inside of her.

She studied his face. His eyes were closed.

She lay in the darkness, studying his face, wondering what she should do, what he would do next.

What he did was take her again, so soon that her heartbeat hadn't even fully quieted from the last. This time his movements were fiercer, more demanding, if such a thing were possible. He was like a wild man, uttering "Laura" through clenched teeth so that her own name sounded faraway. Alien. Wondrous.

Finally, when all was quiet again, he reached

back and pulled the quilt up around them, tucking it behind Laura's back, arranging it up around her ears. "Stay close to me," he said tenderly. "Stay warm."

And then, just before he drifted off to sleep, he whispered sincerely, almost reverently, "Laura Duncan. You are very special."

CHAPTER TWELVE

ADAM AWOKE with sunlight in his eyes. He pressed his chin to his chest to look down the length of his body. He was wrapped in the cocoon of the old quilt, naked inside it, chilled, his shoulder sore.

Then he remembered. He threw the quilt back, sat up and ran his hands through his hair.

Oh, God. Why had he done it? Certainly he'd needed the release, craved it fiercely. The fluid, renewed way his whole body, his brain even, felt this morning was testament to that.

But why, he berated himself, had he chosen a nice woman like Laura Duncan? Now that *he* had come to *her,* what would she expect from him?

In the clear light of the mountain dawn, he had to admit that their coming together didn't feel as if it had anything to do with pity, or with grief. There was only one word for what it felt like— *love.*

He dropped his arms over his drawn-up knees and smiled at the rising sun. The feeling was back. Like rays piercing the sky after a very long cold night. The wanting. The passion. The love.

He twisted and looked behind him, down the mountain at the cabin in the distance. Smoke curled from the chimney. The night's frost had already turned to dew, and he could make out Doc's straw hat and jean jacket as he hoed in the garden.

Where was Laura? What was *she* feeling this morning? When, in the night, had she left him?

He looked around for his clothes and quickly pulled them on. He'd have to find her. Go to her. Make this whole thing right somehow.

AFTER SHE'D LAIN watching Adam's beautiful sleeping face until she thought her heart would break, Laura had carefully slipped free of his embrace. She'd covered him with the quilt and then dressed stealthily in the freezing darkness.

She'd located the flashlight and, alone and heartsick, found her way back down the mountain. In her attic room she'd spent the remaining hours until dawn tossing and turning, trying to make sense of what they'd done.

Okay. She'd gone to bed with her handsome client. Had sex with him.

But no. It was *more* than that. So much more.

What had happened to them? She'd had no idea that lovemaking even existed on that level.

But the truth was that she'd given herself to a sexy man who was still recovering from a terrible accident and still deeply mourning the loss of his wife and child.

Laura sat up on the side of the bed and covered her face in shame. This whole mess was contrary to every value she held dear. And yet...it wasn't. If she had been...carried away, maybe he had been, too. Transported, at least, away from pain and loss and grief. Was that so wrong?

She got up and wandered to the window. The mountain loomed, backlit by the rising sun. "Adam, I'm so sorry," she whispered. "I don't have any excuse for what I've done, except that I...I love you."

And then she began to cry. For all of them. For Elizabeth and Anna and Doc and Katherine. For Adam.

And for herself.

ADAM WALKED STIFFLY back down to the stone house, deciding to give himself time to think before he talked to her. He brewed a pot of coffee, gathered up toiletries, razor and clean clothes and headed for the creek shower.

The frigid water was cathartic. He worked up

a heavy lather and started scrubbing. His hand halted as instinct warned him that someone was watching him. A rush of adrenaline lashed through him.

He quickly rinsed off the soap, then scanned the dense woods around him, the steep bank above. He looked up the creek, then toward the rocky bank on the opposite side. He grabbed his towel. His gun lay on the pile of dry clothes two steps away. He kept his eyes on his surroundings as he reached for it, feeling to make certain the clip was in place.

Gradoff, Toeless had reported only last night, was somewhere in Seattle. But there was no logical way he could have made his way to northern Montana already. Even once he made it to the backcountry, it would take some time to find this place.

In the distance Adam saw something red moving deep in the trees. Laura's jacket! What was she doing up here?

And thinking of Laura and Gradoff in the same instant, it hit him like a rock slide.

He *was* endangering Laura, not only by having her here where Gradoff could find her, but by making love to her, for getting involved with her was endangering her emotionally. How could he go on with his plans when he'd found something to live for—*Laura*. But how could he let Gradoff not pay for what he'd done? And even if he chose to give up the fight, he couldn't be a free man as long as Gradoff and his henchmen were roaming around. There was only one thing to do. He had to get Laura off this mountain.

"Laura!" he called out, but the flash of red was gone.

His disappointment made him more acutely aware of his feelings, of how much he wanted to be with her.

But there were too many things against them right now. He flexed his shoulder. He could do the exercises Laura had taught him on his own. He would send her back. Today. This morning.

LAURA STRUGGLED for breath as she climbed the mountain, up, away from the sight of him. She had to clear her thoughts, decide what to do now. She came to a clearing, sat down on a rock and tried to concentrate, but images of Adam bathing in the creek kept invading. She bit her lip.

He'd grabbed for his gun. She'd scared him, spying on him like that. He must be really afraid if he'd taken a gun with him. Once again, she worried about the Russians.

Suddenly she wished she'd never met Adam Scott. Never heard his voice or gotten to know his tender wounded heart. Never felt his strong arms around her, felt his warm mouth on hers, never felt...

She stood on shaky legs and swallowed.

She had to get away. Today.

ADAM WAS SQUATTING in front of the enormous stone fireplace with his broad back to her. He put a match to the stack of kindling and watched it ignite.

He sighed and his shoulders slumped for a second before he said. "Good morning, Laura."

He stood and faced her.

"We need to talk," she said, knowing her tone sounded, despite her best intentions, sad and frightened.

"Yes, we do." His voice, too, sounded sad.

Laura dived right into the problem. "If what we're doing is right, don't you think we'd both be happy about it?"

Adam frowned. "You're not happy?" It was not so much a question, as a statement of his own fear that she wasn't.

"Of course, I'm not. And look at you, you're not happy, either. This is no way to begin a relationship. You're still grieving and I'm—"

He reached a hand out to her. "Laura stop a minute. You're getting way ahead of yourself here. Okay. Maybe it wasn't the most prudent thing to do, but that doesn't make it wrong.''

She held up a palm. ''Please, let me finish. I don't want a relationship like this—one that gets off on the wrong foot. You told me yourself you couldn't forget them. Well, I don't want to be a stand-in. I don't want to live with some other woman's memory. And I don't want to live with...with your terrible plan to get even.''

Laura had talked so fast that she was positively breathless. The room suddenly seemed close. The fire Adam had lit seemed too bright. Laura rubbed her forehead and staggered.

Adam had his arms around her in an instant. He guided her to the straight-backed chair and made her sit. Then he knelt in front of the chair, the expression on his face one of pure concern. He looked...vulnerable, younger. ''It's not a plan to get even. It's a plan to get justice.''

Laura shook her head. ''Call it what you want, but it's *wrong*. It's more important to you than getting on with your life!''

''Laura, you've got yourself all wrought up,'' he said gently. ''Here. Let me.'' He got up and stood behind her, then rubbed her neck.

So weird, Laura thought, to have him doing the massaging, but it helped. It really did.

When she felt better, she said, ''I like myself

now, Adam, after years of *not* liking myself. And I won't do something, no matter how good it feels in the middle of the night, that might make me stop liking myself.''

She lifted his warm fingers off her neck and got to her feet. ''I'm leaving, Adam. I'm sorry. I hope you'll understand and let me out of the contract. I'll bill you for my normal fee when I get home.''

She took a step, but he blocked her way. His face looked anxious. ''Laura! Are you sure you're not just running away? I mean, you're not going to disappear again or something, are you?''

Laura supposed he'd found out through Toeless all about her disappearance from Dallas. No matter.

''No. I'm not running away. I'm simply taking care of myself. I'm going…home.''

''And that's what I want you to do. I thought about it this morning. But I also don't want to lose you.'' He paused. ''When Toeless and I are finished with this…business, will you come back?''

''I…don't know.''

He nodded. ''I understand. Well, at least you're being honest.'' His tone sounded resigned, final. He turned and walked to the door.

"Please take care of yourself, Laura." He closed the door softly behind him.

Laura folded her arms across her stomach and marched stiffly down the short hall, through the kitchen past Katherine's worried expression, and up the stairs to pack before she could change her mind. This time she was really leaving.

When she came back down the stairs carrying Ned, Katherine said, "What are you doing?"

"I'm going home, Katherine. I'm sorry it's so sudden." Laura gave her an awkward hug, with Ned in the way.

She'd finished packing her things in the car when Doc came to the garden gate and waved. Then he stared in bewilderment as she climbed into the car and started the engine. She saw him in the rearview mirror, standing at the gate with his arms loose at his sides.

And Morton. Dear sweet Morton.

He'd padded along beside her as she'd made each trip back and forth loading her things. Now, as she pulled away, he galloped after the Toyota, barking wildly.

She drove on, but every time she looked in the rearview mirror, he was still behind the car, running and running with his tongue hanging out. Finally she pulled the car close to the rocks at the edge of the road and got out.

Morton trotted up to her and sat on his haunches looking exhausted but happy that she'd finally stopped.

"Morton, go home!" She pointed back up the road.

"Go home!" she repeated more loudly, pointing again.

But the old dog just sat there with the look on his face that always reminded Laura of a smile.

"Go back!" she yelled, and waved her arms.

Morton made a startled feint and gave Laura a hurt, confused look before tucking in his tail and taking a couple of cowering steps in the direction of the homestead.

"Oh, Morton," Laura moaned, and dropped her arms in defeat.

When the dog trotted happily back to her, the dam broke. She dropped to one knee, threw her arms around the dog, laid her cheek against his soft coat and cried.

MOUNTAIN HOME Health Care was a hive of late-afternoon activity: ringing phones, hashing out the next day's assignments, a guest speaker loudly presenting an in-service program in the back room.

The new receptionist, very young, giggled on the phone while two other lines kept ringing.

For a second no else noticed Laura as she sat down at her old desk. Good, she thought. Maybe no one would notice the dark circles under her eyes, her uncharacteristic quietness.

"Laura!" Sylvia Summers said as she came flying into the open area carrying a stack of charts. "What are you doing back? You've got a couple of more weeks of therapy with Mr. Scott."

"He doesn't need me any longer. Everything is basic repetition at this point."

Sylvia's frown deepened. "What's the matter, honey? Did you and Mr. Scott have words? That nasty man didn't have the nerve to fire you, did he?"

"No. I quit. And please, don't ask for details." Laura paged through a file on her desk.

Sylvia shrugged and crossed to the message boxes.

"You've got a stack of messages. None of them urgent, but some lawyer called you. We told him you wouldn't be back for a couple of weeks." Sylvia held out the slips of paper.

Laura took the messages. What now? But when she read the attorney's name, she knew. If the Dallas attorneys were contacting her, it was only a matter of time before Stuart came looking for her.

UP ON THE MOUNTAIN, the next month crawled by slowly. The sun slanted from the south now, and the larch trees were tipped with soft scarlet. The promise of snow touched the air. Doc and Katherine hung around quietly like a pair of old monks attending a broken bird.

"I'm fine," Adam assured them one evening while they were cleaning up the kitchen. "Go back to your house."

"You are not fine," Katherine said. "You are waiting like an angry tiger to do an evil thing."

They'd had this conversation many times in the past few weeks.

"Not evil, Katherine. *Just*. This is justice."

"You don't have to do this for us, you know," Doc said. "We have let Elizabeth and Anna go. They are in the hands of God."

"I'm sure you're right about that. But I have to do this for them."

"Adam, please, just sell the formula," Doc said sensibly. "Or even sell only the prototypes. We know you still have them somewhere. I could help you find several research botanists who specialize in such compounds. Surely one of them could carry on your work."

"It's not only about the formula. Gradoff is a murderer. He has to be stopped before he kills again. Then, when this is over, I'll donate the prototypes to medical science.''

Katherine began to cry. ''I'm sorry,'' she apologized when Doc and Adam both tried to hug her. ''That would make Elizabeth so proud...''

The three fell silent then, remembering Elizabeth, remembering Anna, remembering the gifts—and the love.

LAURA'S FIRST MONTH back at Mountain Home Health Care had been so hectic that she'd lost track of her comings and goings, of her usual routines.

She'd been taking every contract she could get in order to make enough money to be able to pay Stuart back. As a result, she'd been feeling very tired.

At least that was how she'd explained her exhaustion to herself—and to her doctor. But the doctor had insisted on tests. And now Laura knew her exhaustion was not due to overwork.

Though the first light snow of the season had fallen last night, she had decided to walk to clear her head.

The whole town looked quaint and peaceful now, blanketed in a dusting of white. Too early for winter sports. Too late for hiking and fishing. Travel into the wilderness areas would be restricted soon. And Sixteen Mile Creek Road would be closed for the winter.

Laura stopped walking and studied her reflection in the window of a flower shop. Surely Doc and Katherine were looking after him. Should she call him? The tears came then. Laura turned from the glass and swiped at her cheeks with her mittens.

She cut through an alley and got herself off Main Street, away from people, away from the Center Mall. What if she saw someone she knew? She couldn't face anyone from church or work right now, although eventually, she supposed, everyone would know. You couldn't hide a thing like this for long.

She emerged from the alley into the bright sun on a quiet back street. Normally she would have enjoyed the lovely historic buildings she passed, but today she walked the few blocks to Woodland Park absorbed in her thoughts.

She brushed the snow off a bench, sat down with her hands over the prize in her tummy and raised her face to the sun. Was she capable of being a good mother? she wondered.

She sat quietly for a while, daydreaming, fantasizing about her baby, and then she heard shouting coming from a short distance away. Kids on bicycles. Two pink-cheeked little boys all bundled up and pedaling like maniacs, racing each other.

The children turned into the park, gave Laura wide grins as they pedaled past her, plowing through the virgin snow. Out in the open space, they abandoned the bikes and flopped on their backs, whooping and making snow angels.

The boys soon tired of this and hopped back on their bikes. They pedalled off as quickly as they'd appeared.

Laura stood up. Chills ran over her whole body as she stared at the messy snow angels. It felt like a sign. Tears filled her eyes again. Tears of gratitude and wonder.

Little boys. A boy who looked like Adam. How wonderful that would be,

"Laura?" A man's voice from behind her startled her.

The short young man walking jauntily toward her was Reverend Green, the new minister who had recently moved to Kalispell from Missoula. Everybody liked him.

"I thought that was you! Where have you been lately?" He reached out his arms for a brotherly hug. "Have I run you out of church with all my corny jokes?"

"I…" Laura let him hug her, discreetly trying to wipe away her tears, but she knew her glasses were fogged and her nose was red. "I was on a live-in assignment up in the national forest, and lately I've had to work the past few Sundays."

"Wow." He stood back. "A patient up in the national forest? How fascinating. How was that? Living up there?"

Laura's bottom lip trembled. She found she couldn't speak.

Reverend Green had the swift reflexes of a champion gymnast. He pulled her into his arms. "Laura," he soothed, "you're crying. What's wrong? It's not like you to be so upset."

"Oh, Reverend Green!" she sobbed. "I'm pregnant!"

CHAPTER THIRTEEN

WHEN THEY GOT to Laura's house in Reverend Green's Volkswagen, a gray Chevy Lumina was parked in her driveway. A heavy-looking man in a black topcoat and fedora was sitting on Laura's porch swing, his briefcase balanced on his lap, his head bent as he wrote on a piece of paper. He looked up, closed the briefcase and stood.

"You've got company," Reverend Green said.

Laura shivered. She stared at Stuart Hayden Crestwood, trying to decide what to do.

"Laura," Reverend Green touched her arm. "You look pale. That's not...he's not the father of your baby, is he?"

Laura shook her head.

"Do you want me to come in with you?"

She sighed. "No, Reverend. I know you have to get back to work. That man is my ex-husband. I imagine he only wants the twenty-five thousand dollars I stole from him several years ago."

To his credit, the young reverend didn't look

too shocked. "Oh, I see," he said as if this sort of confession was perfectly normal. "Well, Laura, promise to let me know if you need anything. Anything at all."

She nodded and squeezed his arm, then climbed out of the car.

Her boots crunched on the fresh snow as she walked toward Stuart. She stopped at the base of her porch steps and looked up at him. "Hello, Stuart."

"Laura," he said coolly, his Texas drawl dragging her name out in a way that made her shiver. "You're looking...well."

"What are you doing here?" Laura wasn't about to waste breath on hollow amenities, and she wasn't about to invite him into her living room.

"Actually I've come by your home several times in the past few days. I've even been to Mountain Home Health Care. Quaint. People around here are very protective of you, Laura. I was just about to leave you a note."

"How did you find me in the first place? Janie's the only one who knows where I am, and she'd chew her own tongue off before she'd tell you."

"Ah, yes. For once, little Janie managed to keep her trap shut. Except she did let it slip that your mother had relocated to Phoenix with her…fourth husband? Or is he her fifth?''

Laura felt tears sting her eyes, but she fought them back. So her mother had betrayed her. What else was new?

"Your mother is a very practical woman. It can be expensive, living in Phoenix," Stuart continued smoothly.

"What are you doing here?" she repeated.

"We have some unfinished business."

Laura grabbed the knob on the newel post, to brace herself or to control her anger, she wasn't sure which.

"And exactly what would that be?"

"I want to go inside and discuss it."

Laura stood there with her fingers gripping the post. She wanted to say, *I don't give a big green bean what you want, Stuart Crestwood. An hour ago I decided I just might keep the money.*

But she bit her tongue. Fanning the flames of rancor would only cause more trouble. She firmly believed that she was strong enough to handle Stuart now. Maybe they could discuss this calmly, if not amicably.

Yet, as she threw her front door open and let him pass, the idea of being alone in the house with this man gave her a chill. She told herself to remain calm and followed him inside.

"This is nice," Stuart said as he carefully removed his hat, gloves and topcoat and placed them in a neat pile at the end of the couch. Without being invited, he settled himself in the most comfortable-looking chair.

He sighed as he placed his arms on the overstuffed chair arms and looked up at the pressed-tin ceilings of her Victorian house.

"You've done a good job here." He drew a breath and his nostrils flared as he fixed his eyes back on Laura. "Very cozy."

A compliment? From Stuart? "Thank you," she mumbled, and turned away. She removed her parka and hung it on the coat tree, already thinking, *He wants something besides the money, but what?*

"Unfortunately—" Stuart compressed his lips in a pout as he opened his briefcase "—Charlene wasn't so gifted in the domestic area." He took out some papers and put them on the coffee table.

Wasn't? Laura said nothing as she crossed the room to the bay window, deciding to remain standing there in view of the street. "All right," she said calmly, and folded her arms across her chest. "What is this unfinished business?"

"Well, it's no big deal, but your maiden name

is on the deed to some property near downtown Dallas that I bought years ago.''

''What property?''

''Just a small vacant lot. Worthless, no big deal, like I said. I'd almost forgotten it was part of my holdings until my attorney reminded me. That's when we discovered the error.''

''The error?''

''Yes, your name on the deed. I meant it as a kind of...prewedding gift, and—heh-heh—then I forgot about it. The matter should have been cleared up at the time of the divorce.''

It wasn't like Stuart to—heh-heh—forget about anything. ''Stuart, I never knew about this property. How big did you say it was?''

He released a sigh. ''It's small. I simply need you to sign a quit-claim deed over to me so I can dispose of this scrap of land.'' He pulled a pen out of his jacket pocket and picked up the papers.

''How big is it, Stuart?'' Laura enunciated each word.

He shook his head. ''Still as stubborn as ever.'' His tone became impatient, hostile. ''Look, Laura, we need to finalize our affairs. Let's make a deal—I'll forgive the twenty-five thousand you stole from me if you agree to sign the quit-claim deed.''

They would have to negotiate about the money

she owed him, true, but first she needed to know the stakes. "How big is this land?" Laura repeated. "I can always read the deed."

Stuart sighed melodramatically. "Only about three acres," he answered testily.

Laura managed to keep her face turned toward the window. What kind of stunt was Stuart pulling now? What was the real story with this property? She didn't remember being owner of any three acres near downtown Dallas. But then, Stuart had never kept her informed about anything. Surely she had signed something—she rubbed her forehead. Stuart had always been sticking things under her nose: "Sign this, my dear." And she always had. Like a fool.

Well, that had been the old Laura, not the woman who faced him now. "Stuart, three acres near downtown Dallas has got to be worth more than twenty-five thousand dollars. What do you mean when you say you are going to *dispose* of this property?"

He jumped to his feet. "This is why I could never share anything with you regarding finances when we were married. You are an idiot when it comes to money, Laura. Look how you're living." He swept an arm over her humble living room. "A man comes to you and offers to forgive a huge debt, and all you can do is grill him about some worthless piece of property that wasn't even yours in the first place!''

"It wasn't? Then why is my name on the deed?''

"Laura, your name is on the *paper,* but you did not pay for this property. Be fair.''

"Be fair! You call moving nine million dollars to the boonies in order to hide it—'' She stopped, her mouth forming an outraged *O* of understanding. ''Wait a minute! You were trying to *hide* your ownership of this property for some reason, so you put my name on it—my maiden name, to boot.''

Stuart glared at her, his jowls jiggling, his cheeks getting blotchy.

Laura turned her back to him, satisfied that she'd found a way to bargain with him. She kept her voice very calm. "All right, Stuart, when the time comes to sell the property—'' she paused "—and I assume that's what you mean by *disposing* of it, I will pay you the twenty-five thousand from my share of the proceeds.''

For a split second his face was a mask of cold fury, but he quickly changed his expression to a look of genuine concern.

"Laura, honey, this kind of money can be a real burden.''

"Not when you have something meaningful to spend it on," she said with quiet conviction.

"What are you talking about?" Stuart demanded.

Laura drew a deep breath. He might as well understand how deep her motives for opposing him were. "I am expecting a child."

Stuart's eyes widened as he stood there and looked her up and down. Then his fleshy hands balled into fists.

"Pregnant? How can that be? You're *sterile*. For ten years you were completely sterile!"

Laura stepped closer to the window. The postman was sauntering down the street. *Thank goodness.* "A matter of bad chemistry apparently," she said toward the glass. "Obviously, under the right circumstances, I am not sterile. My doctor told me it's rare, but it happens. Look it up."

"You are sterile," he said again, as if repeating the words would make it so.

"I was sterile with *you*, Stuart," she asserted truthfully.

He squinted at her. "You bitch! And to think I came all this way in person, even hoping to perhaps reconcile with you now that Charlene and I are…" He shook his head in disgust. "You managed to get yourself knocked up and now you expect *me* to foot the bill.''

"Get out of my house, Stuart," Laura said calmly. "I have a life now, and I want you out of it."

She grabbed his hat, gloves and topcoat, rolled them into a ball and shoved it into his chest.

"I had intended to pay you back, every dime I owed you, but I see you're still trying to cheat and connive." She pointed at the door. *"Get out!"*

He snatched up his briefcase and left, and a moment later the engine of the Lumina roared to life. It peeled off, spraying muddy snow up the side of her old Toyota.

Laura shuddered, fearing she hadn't seen the last of him.

THE KALISPELL Grand Hotel was like a genteel matron who could make even the pickiest guest feel pampered. But tonight, nothing could please Stuart.

He took a sip of his third gin-and-tonic and seethed. How dare Laura think she could run off with twenty-five thousand dollars! Well, the truth was, for four years he hadn't really cared, but now there was the issue of the land. That land, once developed, would be worth millions, and he didn't intend to have his flaky ex-wife benefit from the deal.

There had to be a way to get her to sign that quit-claim deed and be done with it. She was pregnant! He remembered how foolish she'd always been over babies. This pregnancy had to be useful somehow.

The father.

His detectives had determined that she hadn't remarried, and the dunces had even reported that she was not dating anyone, which was why he'd come up here, deed in hand, like some supplicant.

He'd wanted to see her in the flesh, so to speak. To see if she was still the sexiest woman this side of the Mississippi. A petite Marilyn Monroe, one of his associates had called her.

So. If the detectives hadn't uncovered a relationship, it was probably some kind of secret. A married man perhaps? No, whatever else he thought of his ex-wife, he knew she wasn't the kind to sleep with a married man.

Loud footsteps on the terrazzo floor out in the lobby distracted him. He looked over and saw three young men, possibly students, with backpacks, buzz haircuts and cruel-looking mouths. They were talking to the desk clerk in low voices. One had a foreign accent.

Stuart eavesdropped on their conversation out of sheer boredom—he was the only one left in the bar—but he couldn't make out a word, and he couldn't place the accent.

The young men bade good-night to the desk clerk and headed up the grand oak staircase.

Stuart settled deeper into the leather chair to think.

The father. If the guy had any influence with Laura, *he* might be able to convince her to do the right thing, the simple thing. Or—bright idea!—Stuart could *pay* the father to marry Laura. That would keep her distracted in Montana, away from the quiet-title action that would be necessary if she didn't sign. But court proceedings would take time, and the deal was hot. Stuart needed to sell the land now. Maybe the father, with some encouragement, would convince Laura to sign.

All that remained now was to find the father. That was doable, provided he fired his old detectives and hired sharper ones. It shouldn't take more than a couple of days. Stuart relaxed. He signaled the waiter for another round.

CHAPTER FOURTEEN

THE INVESTIGATION was swift and painless. Stuart told the new detective to start at Mountain Home Health, based on some interesting information from the old detective: Laura had recently returned from a long live-in assignment in the Kootenai National Forest.

Thanks to a talkative young receptionist, the detective determined that the patient was a difficult reclusive man—"Adam," the girl had let slip over the phone. From there Stuart had put two and two together. An affair with a patient?

But for two days Stuart got no closer to the truth. Then a bit of luck befell him.

He was eavesdropping on the foreign students again during the continental breakfast when the name "Adam" caught his attention. He listened intently. They were talking in very low voices about someone who had gone into hiding, someone named Schneider. They were speculating—and here was the really exciting part—about the extent of his "recovery." Then they lapsed into a foreign tongue. But now Stuart had a name.

"Get Mountain Home Health's phone records. I don't care how you do it." The detective had complied, and the records showed many calls, to and from the same remote exchange.

Stuart settled against the headboard of the Victorian bed and waited for someone to answer the phone.

"Hello." An elderly woman's voice.

"May I speak to Adam Schneider please?"

A very long silence.

"Who is calling?" She sounded shaky.

"My name is Stuart Crestwood, ma'am. I'm a friend of Laura Duncan's."

A sharp intake of air. Then, "Is Laura all right?"

"Oh, Laura's fine. But I need to ask Mr. Schneider a question. Is he there?"

"One minute."

KATHERINE CAREFULLY PLACED the receiver on top of the wall unit. Had she used the name Schneider when she'd told Laura the story? She rubbed her forehead. Damn this old brain. She went to get Adam.

Stuart waited on the line for what seemed a

millennium. Then a strong baritone voice said, "Who is this?"

"Mr. Schneider?"

"I asked you first. Who is this?"

"I'm sorry. Adam, then?"

"What do you want?"

"I am Stuart Hayden Crestwood. Laura Duncan's ex-husband. I understand you know her? She was your therapist?"

"What do you want with Laura?"

Ah, Stuart thought, a note of protectiveness. "Mr.... Perhaps I was misinformed about your name."

"Depends. Who did the informing?"

"I overheard it. But the speaker had an accent. I could have misunderstood."

Adam mulled this over. Perhaps Crestwood was staying at the Kalispell Grand. "Three young guys? One wearing glasses?" he said.

"Why, yes."

This might be handy. "You didn't misunderstand them, Mr. Crestwood. Schneider is my name. But I use an alias now." This was probably going to be too easy. Something would go wrong, Adam's gut warned him. But by the time Gradoff and crew made the long drive up here, Katherine and Doc would be safely home. And that was one good thing about Laura's returning to Kalispell. The only good thing.

"Oh. Well. I figured it was something like that." Crestwood's voice sounded too blasé. "I will be discreet, Mr. Schneider. In fact, I believe we can help each other," he went on. "That is why I called."

"Go on."

"I spoke with Laura a couple of days ago and she seems to think highly of you. Very highly."

What is this? Adam thought. Laura wouldn't discuss their relationship with anybody. Of course, he'd never told her the whole truth. She could have innocently divulged something. "And?"

"And I was hoping you could talk some sense into her."

"Depends upon what you mean by *sense*. What is it you want?"

"There are some legal problems stemming from our divorce," Stuart said, "and I need Laura's signature on an old title. If she doesn't give me her signature voluntarily, I'll be forced to file suit in Dallas to clear that title. I called you because I thought that surely you don't want her involved in a nasty lawsuit, traveling back and forth to Texas, in her condition."

"Her condition?"

"Yes, her condition. You don't know?"

"Know what?"

Stuart paused. He hoped to hell he was right about this man being the father. "Mr. Schneider, Laura claims that you're about to become a father. Or is that another one of her little... stories?"

"Are you telling me Laura is pregnant?"

"She told me so herself."

Adam didn't respond. He was too busy trying to absorb this incredible news. Laura was pregnant! They'd only made love twice!

"Laura...well, Laura has her pride," Stuart continued, "but she did indicate that she has some financial problems."

There was a stony silence on the line. Static crackled while Adam tried to think what this guy was really up to. He hoped it was only money. Money he could manage. Easily.

"Crestwood, you'd better not be lying to me."

"I'm not. I can't imagine why Laura hasn't told you the news herself—" Stuart stopped abruptly. Suddenly he could imagine all kinds of reasons.

"Just tell me what you want."

Stuart sensed an advantage. This man's tone of voice said he was willing to risk something. Furthermore, why was he living in such an isolated place? Under an assumed name? Maybe there was more to be gained here than simply a signature on a deed. Stuart had been prepared to *offer* money, but maybe he'd misread the situation.

"I've told you what I want. Laura's signature on a quit-claim deed. There is another pressing matter, though. Laura owes me a great deal of money. And in her delicate condition—" Stuart said the phrase so as to make it abundantly clear that exposing the pregnancy was the consequence of refusal "—she's naturally worried about her ability to pay me back."

WHEN ADAM HUNG UP the phone, his first thought was that, with Stuart Crestwood in the vicinity, Laura might run away again.

And he couldn't let her go.

He turned to Doc and Katherine, who'd huddled in the hallway listening in on the conversation. The man's use of the name Schneider, he supposed, had spooked them.

He held up his palms. "Everything's okay," he said.

"Everything's okay?" Katherine challenged and charged forward. "I hear you say Laura's pregnant and everything's okay?"

"Katherine, hush." Doc came up behind his

wife and cupped her shoulders. "That part is none of our business. We are concerned about Gradoff," he told Adam. "I couldn't believe my ears. You told that man, whoever he was, that your real name was Schneider."

"I know what I'm doing. Now listen to me. You must gather up your things and go back to your own house. Don't come back up here." Adam looked at the clock. "It'll be dark soon. I'll come down and check on you in a little while. I need to borrow some things."

Doc and Katherine exchanged worried frowns.

"Don't worry about me. Now hurry up and pack. I've got to call Toeless."

Adam moved to the phone and punched out his friend's cell-phone number.

"There's a way to speed things up," he said as soon as Toeless answered. "We can make sure they find me sooner. Did you know Laura's ex-husband is at the Kalispell Grand Hotel, too?…My thoughts exactly. We can use this guy to deliver the message to the Russians. It shouldn't be hard. We have something he wants. But before we use him, I've got to take care of something more important. Detain Crestwood, make sure he doesn't talk to anyone for the next twenty-four hours. I don't really care how. I'll check back with you when I get to town…Yes,

I'm coming to town...Never mind why...Yeah, I'll be in disguise."

LAURA WIPED HER HANDS on the dish towel she was holding, snapped on her porch light, looked out and opened the door.

A man in a knitted toque and aviator sunglasses stood on her porch.

"Laura," he said in a deep voice.

It was Adam.

She clamped a hand over her mouth, then grabbed the front of his ski jacket and dragged him inside. "What in the name of God are you doing here?" she cried.

He held up his palms placatingly. "Laura, please hear me out."

"You shouldn't be seen," she hissed, violently tugging the lace curtains in her living room closed.

"I know, but I had to see you."

"You could get killed!"

"How do you know that?" He took off the sunglasses and stared at her.

"Katherine told me...everything. Some time ago. About the Russians. About the key-man insurance. About the formula, the prototypes."

Adam felt like he'd been punched in the gut.

He sank onto the little settee facing the fireplace. "So you know the accident wasn't an accident?"

"Yes." Laura sat down beside him. Her brow was furrowed and her blue eyes radiated compassion. "And I am so sorry, Adam."

"Listen, Laura," he said after a moment. "It's okay that you know everything. I was planning to tell you the whole story myself as soon as..." He stopped.

Laura waited for him to continue. After which, she planned to tell him how wrong he was.

But instead, he said, "We've got a problem. Your ex-husband called me."

"Stuart! What on earth was Stuart doing calling you?"

"He wants something."

She was gripped with a sudden apprehension, as always happened when Stuart was involved. What could he want from Adam? Her shoulders slumped as the energy drained from her. What had Stuart told Adam? That was the really troubling question. "What did he want?" she asked softly.

"You, I suspect, deep down."

"Me?"

He shrugged. "Yeah. I'm just guessing, but he seemed too interested in—if you ask me, too jealous of—our relationship for a man who's really through with a woman.''

"Oh, he's through with me, all right, whether he knows it or not.'' She stood up, too incensed by Stuart's audacity to sit still. She paced to the fireplace, wringing the dish towel in her hands.

"He claimed he wanted you to sign a quit-claim deed on some property.''

She whirled around. "I told him I wouldn't do it.''

"Why not?''

"Why not? Adam, he hid *millions* from me at the time of our divorce. All right, I made off with some money to start my life over, but...'' Laura looked down at him, her eyes imploring. "How can I ever make a man like you understand a man like Stuart Crestwood? You can't imagine...''

Their eyes met, and Laura saw his understanding as plainly as she'd seen his love that first night in the stone house. "I understand guys like Stuart better than you think," he said. "What I can't imagine is a woman like you living with a creep like that for one day, much less ten years.''

Laura nodded in acknowledgement. "I'm not sure I understand it myself.'' She paused and sighed. "Anyway, I always intended to pay the money back, but first I needed to finish school.

I don't have anyone, no one in this world, that I can count on besides myself.''

"No family?'' Adam said. He suddenly realized that Katherine probably knew more about Laura's background than he did. He'd been too wrapped up in his own problems to get to know her. *But give me a chance, Laura. Give me a chance and I'll spend the rest of my life getting to know you.*

Laura shook her head. "I don't even know who my real father is. My mom's been married so many times I've lost count. She lives in Phoenix somewhere. I call her once a year. The standard holiday chat. My grandmother was my only real family.''

"Was?'' Adam said gently.

"She died just before I married Stuart.''

"Ah,'' Adam breathed, then frowned. "So that's why you married the creep.''

"Anyway, I've made myself a new life here and I love it. You've got to understand how different my world is now from the one I had with Stuart. I'm proud of everything I've accomplished.''

"You have every reason to be,'' Adam said. "I think you're a wonderful person, Laura. I'm sure your friends think so, too.''

"I have a lot of love in my life. I love my

friends, my work, my hobbies. I even love my patients.'' Here she stopped, and he saw her cheeks pinken.

Laura cleared her throat and continued. ''Not long after I started working at Mountain Home Health, your case came up. I'll be honest with you—I didn't exactly relish the idea of going up on that mountain after the way the nurses talked about you.''

''Ah, yes.'' Adam smiled. ''The deranged Mr. Scott.''

She didn't smile back. ''The high fee you were willing to pay would have allowed me to pay off Stuart and free myself from my past with him.''

''You're already free of him,'' Adam assured her quietly.

''Not really. I'll never be free of Stuart until he hasn't got any reason to hunt me down and poison my new life.''

''Then why not sign the quit-claim deed?''

Laura frowned and picked a fingernail. ''For one thing I need the leverage…now. I want him to sell the land and let me call twenty-five thousand of the proceeds mine. He'll get to keep that money, of course. But I need him to know that he can't just come in and make demands. Even after four years he's trying to control my life.

Someone needs to teach him a lesson. So even if he makes legal trouble..."

"He won't make trouble, Laura. He won't make any kind of trouble."

His protective tone caused a lump to form in her throat. "How can you know that?"

He got up and stood before her at the fireplace, and something in his posture, something guarded, told her that he was afraid to tell her how he knew.

"Adam, did he say something else bad about me?"

"No. He... I'll take care of him."

"How?" Laura didn't understand.

"I know his kind well. I deal with them all the time. For them, money—no matter the amount—represents power. Now that he knows where you live, he wouldn't have given you a moment's peace—until he had his money back *and* your signature on that deed."

Adam picked up the fire poker and dropped to one knee, prodding the logs in the fireplace. The flames leaped back to life.

"*Had* his money back?" Laura questioned.

"Don't worry. I took care of it." Adam hung the poker in the rack and stood.

"You took care of what?"

"The money. I'm paying him off. He'll probably make the draw tomorrow. After I make the authorization call. I told him to wait for word at his hotel. I needed to talk to you first. I wanted to make sure he hadn't scared you off, run you out of town.''

Laura stared at him while he spoke. When she finally said something, it wasn't the words of gratitude he'd anticipated.

"How dare you!" she exploded. "My debts are none of your business! I don't need some rich man to rescue me. Don't you realize how hard I've worked to make myself independent?"

"Laura, I don't blame you for taking some of that creep's money when you did. A court of law might agree. But now he won't bother you again."

She stood with both hands fisted at her sides. "I'd like you to leave."

"Leave? Laura!" He grabbed her arm. She wrenched it free.

"Yes," she hissed. "Go. You're no better than Stuart. Just another rich man playing chess with people's lives. Deduct my entire salary from what you paid him. I'll find some way to reimburse you for the rest."

"Would you forget about the money?" he yelled.

"I don't want your money, Adam Scott," she

yelled back. "Even if it does ease your conscience after sleeping with me!"

At the look of stunned injury on his face, her attitude softened.

"I didn't mean that. I...I've been so emotional lately. Adam," she added much more quietly, "you're wasting your money. That won't satisfy Stuart. There's still the matter of the property."

"I know." Adam looked at her sincerely. "He wanted *me* to convince you to sign the paper. And I think you should. Just sign over the deed and get rid of the guy."

"You? Why did he think you could convince me to do that?"

"Because..." Adam's eyes grew misty. It took him a moment to go on. When he did speak, his lips curved in a soft hopeful smile. "Because it seems I'm the father of your baby."

Laura's heart sank. She lowered herself into the settee. "Stuart told you about the baby," she whispered.

Adam sat down next to her. He imprisoned her hands tenderly in his own. "So it's true? You're sure?"

She nodded.

"Oh, God." Adam leaned forward and pressed her knuckles to his lips. "I can't believe it."

"I'm sorry you had to find out this way."

"Laura, I think Stuart's using your pregnancy made me hate him more than anything. Maybe he assumed I already knew." He tightened his grip when she tried to pull away. "You should have told me first."

Laura felt as if she couldn't breathe. "I only found out myself a few days ago," she choked out. "You can't imagine what a surprise it is. I...I always thought I was sterile. When I was married to Stuart, I didn't use birth control for ten years and nothing happened."

"Maybe that's what's stuck in his craw. Something sure is. But forget him. This is about you and me. And this baby. How do you feel about it?" He squeezed her hands.

"Scared," she said in a small voice. "But incredibly happy," she added in a stronger one.

"Why are you scared?"

She looked at him as if he'd lost his mind. "Any woman facing raising a baby alone would be scared."

"Why do you think you'll be alone?" He raised an eyebrow.

Laura slid her hands out of his and stood. "No, Adam."

"What do you mean, *no*?"

"If I didn't want to have a relationship with

you as some kind of substitute, I certainly don't want to have a relationship with you because I'm pregnant. I told you, I want the real thing.''

"Who says we can't have the real thing? Laura, all I've thought about since you left is *you*.''

"Really?'' she challenged. "You haven't thought about getting even with Gradoff?''

Adam opened his mouth to speak, then pressed his lips firmly together.

Yes, Laura thought, *we did agree to be honest.* "I'm sorry, Adam. I still have too many mistakes from my past to clean up. Don't authorize that check,'' she said softly. "I'll find a way to deal with Stuart on my own.'' She stared into the fire. "And you have too many…'' She almost said "ghosts,'' but was glad she stopped herself short of that insensitivity. "You have too many issues right now. Let's just give it a little time.''

He hung his head, and Laura felt a tremendous wave of guilt as she looked down at the top of his beautiful thick hair. She should never have gotten involved with this man.

CHAPTER FIFTEEN

"I UNDERSTAND YOU'RE WAITING for word from Mr. Adam Schneider."

Stuart lowered his newspaper and scrutinized the man standing in the hotel lobby before him. He instantly judged him to be a rough biker type. Stuart had noticed a few of those up here. They probably worked in the logging industry. The hokey black eye patch made Stuart want to smirk, but because this man had mentioned Schneider, he smiled pleasantly instead.

"And you are?"

"Toeless Elko. I work for Adam. Don't get up." The big man lowered himself into the matching wing chair on Stuart's right.

Stuart didn't care how crude this man was, he was glad to see him, because when they finished their business, Stuart Hayden Crestwood was getting out of this backwoods town. Last night he'd been detained—for hours—by the local police for driving under the influence. For pity's sake. Two gin-and-tonics. He hadn't been familiar with the controls in the rental car, that was all.

"I'm supposed to give you this." Elko reached into the pocket of his dirty camouflage jacket and drew out a white envelope with a local bank's logo in the corner.

Stuart laid his newspaper aside and glanced around the lobby. He wet his lips and took the envelope. The paper seemed to crackle too noisily as he opened it. He withdrew a cashier's check, drawn on a local bank, for twenty-five thousand dollars. Purchaser: Adam Scott.

Scott? Stuart was puzzled for a second, then he remembered about the alias.

"The blue carbon please." The large man held out his hand.

Stuart tore the back copy off and handed it to Elko. The deal, apparently, was done.

The man folded the carbon carefully and put it into his pocket. "Mr. Schneider also told me that you have a deed you want signed."

Stuart eyed the stranger. But he supposed if this oaf was delivering cashier's checks, he was legitimate. "I want Laura Duncan to sign it, yes."

"Adam said to tell you that he thinks he can make that happen, provided you do him one small favor."

Stuart was listening closely now.

"Go over to the courtesy phone. Ask the desk to connect you to Toly Gradoff. That's one of the Russian students staying here at the hotel."

Russian? What sort of people had Laura gotten herself mixed up with? Only the prospect of getting his hands firmly on that land gave Stuart fortitude.

"When he answers," Elko continued, "and he will—he's there, I checked—tell him you happened to overhear him talking about Adam Schneider."

Stuart nodded.

"Ask him, is that the same Adam Schneider who is Bill Schneider's boy—Bill Schneider, the California developer? When he says yes, tell him you've known Adam a long time, and isn't it a small world, and how does Toly happen to know him? You know, friendly bullshit like that. Use that good-old-boy Texas drawl of yours. Then he'll feed you a load of crap back. Say, isn't that somethin'? Then ask him if he'd mind meeting you at the Moosehead Saloon down the street at eight o'clock for a drink."

Stuart thought, what the hell? He knew he was staring at the man, trying to absorb all of this. In his many years of doing business, shady and otherwise, he'd seen some pretty strange ducks, but this guy took the prize.

"Go on. Make the call, then come back here."

TOELESS WAITED while Stuart placed the call. Five minutes later Stuart was back, looking a little sweaty. Toeless smiled.

"What'd he say?"

"He seemed delighted to have made the connection, actually. He said he and his friends are former students of Adam's and that they're touring Yellowstone and Glacier and wanted to look Adam up while they were this far north, but they hadn't had any luck finding him." Stuart leaned forward in his chair. "What is all this lying about?"

"Take it easy." Toeless gave him a contemptuous glance. "You've done more lying than anybody."

Stuart flopped back in the chair and placed a palm on his chest, heaving a strained sigh. "Do you think they'll show up at the Moosehead?"

"They will. And I'll be at the next table to make sure you say exactly what I tell you to say."

Stuart swallowed, then picked up his coffee cup with a shaky hand and sipped. "What is it you want me to say?"

"That you'll be leaving town tomorrow and you're wondering if they'd mind delivering a gift to Adam. An item for the cabin. You stayed there as a guest last year. You'd deliver it yourself, but you simply don't have time. Adam's dad gave you a map to their land in the national forest. You'll say, too bad the phones up there are out. Got it?"

"I hope I can do this," Stuart said, now clearly nervous.

"You can. The main thing is to give them the map."

"You are certain Schneider can get Laura's signature?"

"Hey. Adam's a can-do guy. You've got a big fat cashier's check in your pocket, haven't you?"

"I KNEW IT HAD TO BE something like that," Sylvia Summers said as she and Laura rounded the corner of First and Main.

The old downtown area was already looking festive, with thousands of tiny white lights and even a few early Christmas decorations in the picturesque shops and restaurants.

"For one thing, today was the first time I've ever known you to cancel a patient appointment." Sylvia shook her head. "You certainly haven't been yourself lately, especially the last three days.''

"That's how long I've known." Laura took a huge breath of the chilly night air and released it in a white cloud. "I feel so much better now that I've told you. Thanks for taking me to dinner, Sylvia."

Sylvia smiled. "My pleasure. So, now what?"

"I'll have a sweet little baby soon. I couldn't ask for anything more."

They walked half a block in silence. Laura's chest felt tight. She *could* ask for more. She could ask for Adam.

Main Street in Kalispell was crowded tonight, despite the snow and freezing temperatures of recent days. People hurried along the sidewalks, and milled in and out of cafés and steak houses, looking for warmth and food. Both theaters had long lines of couples in fleece hats and quilted parkas, stamping their boots in the new snow. Laura looked away.

"Adam Scott." Sylvia shook her head again. "Laura, I hate to say it, but how could you..."

"Sleep with a man like that? Because he's not like that. He's courageous and he's smart and he's—"

"Don't tell me you're in love with him!" Sylvia stopped right there on the sidewalk.

"Shh." Laura looked around at the passersby. Then something across the street caught her eye and she gripped Sylvia's arm. "Omigosh!"

"What is it?" Sylvia followed Laura's shocked gaze.

"It's Toeless Elko and my ex-husband going into the Moosehead Saloon together."

By the time Sylvia adjusted her bifocals, the men were already inside the door. "Who's... Did you say *Toeless*?"

"He's Adam's best friend. Some kind of private investigator. What is Toeless doing with Stuart? That can't be a coincidence." She grabbed Sylvia's arm. "Come on." She pulled her friend across the street.

When Laura peeked in the corner of the tavern's front window, she spotted Toeless and Stuart sitting at separate tables off in a corner, back-to-back. Stuart still had his topcoat on.

"That guy came into the office asking about you," Sylvia said when she saw where Laura was looking.

"Which one?"

Sylvia tilted her chin down to peer over her glasses. "Well, actually, both of them!"

Laura frowned at Sylvia. "Figures." When she looked back into the smoky bar, three young men—two resembling body builders and a skinny one with glasses—were taking seats at Stuart's table. "What the heck?" she said softly.

For a moment they appeared to be having a social conversation. Then they all leaned forward, their postures instantly tense as Stuart handed the one wearing the glasses a package and a piece of paper.

Before the waitress even came back with their drinks, the younger men stood up and left in a hurry.

They burst out the door of the bar and stopped in the middle of the sidewalk not far from where Laura and Sylvia were standing. Their breath rolled out in clouds of steam as they engaged in a heated discussion—in Russian.

Laura had to fight to control her breathing.

The young men moved on, crossing the street. Laura peeked back into the bar.

She saw Stuart stand up and don his fedora. Toeless was punching out a number on his cell phone.

Laura pulled Sylvia to the window of the art gallery next door. "I may need to borrow your Jeep," she said quietly, urgently, as she pretended to admire the watercolors on display. "Can Harvey come down here and pick you up?"

Sylvia studied Laura's profile. "Laura, what the hell is this?"

"Please," Laura begged. "You know I wouldn't ask if it weren't crucial."

Sylvia took her keys out of her pocket. "Please take care," she said.

"Thanks." Laura grabbed the keys and dashed into the bar.

"Toeless!" she hissed as she charged up to his table. "Those guys—" she pointed toward the plate-glass window "—are the Russians!" The men were getting into a black Ford Expedition parked across the street.

Toeless said, "Hold on, Adam," calmly into the cell phone. He gave Laura a level look. "I know that."

Laura stood there, staring at him in horror as comprehension struck. "Oh, God," she said as a sickening rush of adrenaline surged from her gut to her head.

"I will not let him do this!" she cried in a shrill voice that carried over the bar music. "Give me that phone!" She grabbed at it.

Toeless jerked away and in the tussle knocked his chair over. He backed up, not wanting to hurt Laura, but she came at him like a badger and wrestled the phone from his hand.

She put it to her ear. "Adam!" Then she

stared at it. The power button had been punched off in the fight.

"Toeless, tell me his number!"

The Moosehead barflies were gawking.

"Laura, let's go somewhere quiet so I can explain this."

"Go to hell! Katherine was right. You *are* bad for Adam." Still clutching his phone, Laura turned on her heel and bolted from the bar.

It wasn't until she was in Sylvia's Jeep that it dawned on her that she could simply turn on the phone and punch Redial.

Adam picked up immediately. "Toeless? What the hell happened?"

"I won't let you do this."

"Laura? How—"

"I'm coming up there," she continued.

"No, Laura," he said smoothly. "Don't."

"I know what you're planning to do," she replied. She pulled the Jeep out into the plodding traffic of Main Street. "And I can't let you do it. I love you too much." Her eyes misted as she studied the cell phone's buttons. She blinked to clear the tears and punched Off.

CHAPTER SIXTEEN

THE CELL PHONE rang repeatedly on the long trip up Highway 93. Adam. Or perhaps even Toeless, but Laura didn't answer it. Somewhere out on this highway with her were three young men, driving to their deaths. Maybe they *were* evil, she thought as the Jeep's headlights clipped past the tall pine trees, maybe they deserved to die, but not at Adam's hand. She would not let him destroy his soul for vengeance. If she could get there before the Russians—and she could, using the shortcut—she might talk Adam out of this, plead with him, get him to call in the police.

She was halfway there when it started to snow again. The phone had stopped ringing by the time she turned onto Sixteen Mile Creek Road, and the snow had gotten much heavier. She could see lights in the windows of Doc and Katherine's house, and she prayed that meant they were safe inside. As the Jeep bucked up the steep rocky shortcut, Laura muttered, ''Forgive me, Sylvia,'' and hoped she would have enough time.

When she pulled up in the snow-packed drive-way, Adam was standing outside the darkened cabin with the night-vision binoculars dangling in one hand.

He'd been up in the attic, she knew, and had probably watched her turn off the highway, then take the shortcut.

She jumped from the Jeep and rushed at him. "I will not let you do this!" she screamed.

Adam dropped the binoculars, grabbed her and spun her around, pinning her backside against his body with one viselike arm while he roughly frisked her with the other. As Laura struggled against him, he yanked down the zipper of her parka, jammed his big hand inside, feeling everywhere, then produced the cell phone from her inside pocket.

"Great!" he said as he clutched it in an angry fist in front of her face. "Now Toeless can't talk to me!"

"I don't want him to!" Laura wailed as she wrenched free of his hold. "I want you to stop this! Right now!"

"You shouldn't have come up here, Laura," he said coldly as he picked up the binoculars and peered down the mountain.

"I had to!" she cried. "I'm trying to stop you

from doing something you'll regret for the rest of your life!''

"I won't regret it," Adam said, and lowered the binoculars. "Come on. They'll be here soon."

He jerked her around to the back of the cabin where a snowmobile sat waiting, bow and arrows strapped to its side.

"You'll stay in the stone house. When they follow the snowmobile's tracks up, and they will, I'll be waiting at the edge of the clearing."

"No! Adam, at least let me be with you," she pleaded.

Adam threw his leg over the seat and mounted the machine. "No. I'd leave you down here, but they'd get their hands on you. I'll stop them before they make it to the stone house. Get on!" he shouted as he fired up the engine. He gave Laura a hand up and turned his head as she clasped his back. "Lean in the same direction as I do."

Adam cut a rough path through the trees, hugging the side of the mountain as they zigzagged up to the stone house.

"Won't they know I'm here when they see Sylvia's Jeep?" Laura asked when they were inside the cabin.

"They'll know at least two people are up here

somewhere,'' Adam said calmly as he unzipped a subzero sleeping bag and opened it on the bed. "But since that's not your Toyota…" He pointed into the flannel-lined envelope. "Get in."

Laura was shivering, but she didn't move toward the bed. "I want you to give it to them, Adam."

"Give what to them?"

"The formula and the prototypes," Laura said.

His dark eyes flicked—once—up over her shoulder to the wild-iris print. "Get in the sleeping bag, Laura. Now."

"No. Katherine told me they'll sell it on the black market and get their profit that way. It's not worth dying for." As she said this, Laura tried to read his eyes for some sign that the man she loved was in there, that the father of her child hadn't completely lost touch with what was good, with what was sane.

He grabbed her arm. "And what do you think the people they sell it to are going to do with it? Make cough drops? Did Katherine happen to tell you they'll use it to gain advantage in biological warfare? Huh? Did she? Dammit, Laura. These men will kill us even if I *do* give them the formula. Don't you understand that?"

He scooped her up in his arms and threw her onto the sleeping bag. She struggled with him, but he pushed her shoulders down. "Laura!" he said through clenched teeth. "Don't make this worse than it already is!"

"Adam, please—" Laura started, but he clamped his hand over her mouth, his eyes suddenly wide.

"Listen."

The sound of a motor down at the big cabin froze her. Adam pushed her down again and this time she allowed him to zip her into the sleeping bag.

"Lie still," he said. "And do not come out of this house, no matter what you hear."

LAURA'S HEART POUNDED as she lay in the dark listening to the sound of Adam making a lot of noise with the snowmobile out in the clearing.

Then the motor stopped.

Several minutes of eerie silence passed, and then she heard something—thrashing in the trees. About the same time she saw a light flashing past the small windows.

Low voices, speaking in Russian, caused her to sit up. She heard a sudden "Ugh!" followed by gunshots and loud shouts in Russian.

Had Adam hit one of them with an arrow?

Even more frightening—had one of them shot Adam with a gun?

No sooner had she finished that thought than someone kicked the door open and blinding light filled the room.

While one man dragged a body inside, another man, a skinny one, followed him and slammed the door shut, then plastered himself beside the window with a rifle poised at his shoulder.

The man who dragged the body stopped and shone the light on Laura. "Don't move," he said in unaccented English, then flicked it off. Even in the darkness, Laura could tell he was hunched over the body. He mumbled something in Russian. The thin man by the window replied, and the huge man stood and stationed himself by the other window. The room fell silent.

After several watchful moments the thin man crossed to Laura in three heavy steps and jerked her upright, sleeping bag and all, and shone the white beam of a halogen flashlight into her face. "What is on the arrows?" he asked with no trace of an accent. Laura looked at the body lying as still as death on the floor. She gasped in horror.

"Shouldn't we ask her about the formula?" the other said from the darkness, also in perfect English. She'd assumed they'd all sound like evil spies in a Cold War movie. But their voices sounded young, fresh.

The thin man moved his face forward out of the shadows. "Ms. Duncan." His glasses glinted as he spoke. "My name is Toly."

Gradoff.

Laura wondered fleetingly how he knew her name.

He slipped his stocking cap off as if being polite—and adjusted the strap of the semiautomatic rifle over his shoulder.

"We are sorry to frighten you. We mean you personally no harm, but Mr. Schneider has stolen something that belongs to us. You will tell us anything you know that might help us reclaim it. It is most urgent. We mean you no harm," he repeated, and made a gesture with his hand. The other man began searching the room.

Laura was careful not to let her eyes stray to the print of the wild iris as she sat there in the sleeping bag. Did this mean they only wanted the formula and the prototypes? But she swallowed when she thought of what Adam had said about biological warfare.

"Where is Schneider?" Gradoff asked quietly as he leaned toward her, his face partially in the beam of the halogen light. He was so slender, so young-looking. His buzz haircut and the wide eyes behind the rimless glasses made him seem vulnerable. The oblique light accentuated his bad skin and made his lips look almost purple. His breath stank of alcohol.

She turned her head. "I don't know who you're talking about."

"Mr. Schneid— Ah, yes, I believe you know him as Mr. Scott."

"My boss?" Laura stalled as she fumbled for the inside tab on the zipper of the sleeping bag. "As far as I know, he's not here."

"She's lying," the large man said. "Listen, pretty girl—" The sound of the snowmobile roaring away outside stopped him. Both he and the skinny man rushed to a window and let fly with gunfire at the escaping snowmobile.

Laura started shaking so hard during the barrage that she was amazed she could maneuver the zipper. But she did.

When the shooting stopped, the two men exchanged glances. "I say we leave Lipki and track Schneider," the big one said. "He's probably got the formula on him."

"No," Gradoff said. "We wait here. He'll come back for her." He cut a glance at Laura.

Through a great effort of will, she kept her eyes wide, confused-looking, trained on Gradoff's. She desperately needed a diversion.

"Why do you need Mr. Scott? He keeps all his scientific stuff on his laptop—right over there." She nodded her head at a pile of dirty clothes on the coffee table.

Gradoff stared at her, then swiveled his head in the direction she pointed. He crossed the room to the table and began to fling the clothes aside, then squatted down and raised the screen on the laptop. Meanwhile Laura cautiously finished working the zipper down.

Gradoff turned the computer on and started furiously clicking the keyboard. The other man stood behind him, intently studying the screen. She would have only seconds to get through the door…

The skinny one spit out something that sounded like a curse, then slammed the laptop closed.

"I still say we can go after him," the large one said confidently, "if we use her as a shield." The fact that he had spoken in English seemed doubly terrifying. They weren't even hiding their intentions now.

She was glad she was fully dressed for the weather when the large one hauled her out of the sleeping bag and dragged her outside. She wondered how much cold her baby could endure.

Please, she prayed, *don't let my child be hurt.*

Avoiding the moonlit expanse of snow, they took her into the shadowy spruce trees at the edge of the clearing.

"We follow the snowmobile tracks," the big one said. "Stay close behind me." He held Laura tightly against him with one arm as he shoved her along and aimed the flashlight at the tracks.

When they got deeper into the woods, the snow grew uneven, drifted in places, feeling like quicksand as they got closer to the place where the cornice of rock jutted out over the creek.

She feared they were going straight up to Adam's vantage point. But that was what Adam wanted, wasn't it? To have them directly in the line of his arrows again.

CHAPTER SEVENTEEN

LAURA DIDN'T HAVE TIME to worry about what Adam would do for long. As they came up alongside the creek, her captor brought her up short.

"That's a wild creek," he muttered in her ear. "Dangerous. A person could drown."

Behind them, Gradoff hissed something in Russian and the big man laughed.

What had Katherine told her? That they would have to make Adam's death look like an accident? And once they got the formula, would they make hers look accidental, too?

The big one's gun was slung over his shoulder, she knew; she didn't know about Gradoff's. But running might be her only chance of survival. And if she ran now, maybe they would have to split up to look for her. Then Adam would have his opportunity.

The Russian shoved Laura along as the path suddenly rose, dropping off to the right into a deep snow-filled gully. When he leaned back as she stepped up onto a rock, she found her chance. She reared sharply back, causing him to lose his balance and fall backward onto Gradoff. As both men went sliding into the gully, Laura broke free and ran for the trees.

She climbed frantically, her breath coming in loud rasps as she clawed uphill in the snow, leaving their shouts behind. Her hands felt frozen.

She knew she was near the rock cornice. Where the moonlight broke through the trees, she could see surprisingly well, and she veered off the path in exactly the right spot.

She stopped short of stepping up onto the rock outcropping and took a mad second to clump around in the snow, making a mess of her trail. She thrashed off the path in a false direction, ran in a circle around a big larch, closing the loop of churned snow, making it look as if she'd doubled back.

The branch she remembered was just low enough to grab.

The sound of the men's voices farther down the mountain spurred her on. She jumped up and grasped the low limb. With the bark scraping her palms, she worked herself along, hand over hand, like a kid on a jungle gym, being careful not to disturb the mantle of snow just below her toes. When her feet dangled beyond the edge of the cornice, she thought of her baby and prayed the drifts had gotten deep enough to cushion her fall. Then she dropped like a stone.

She hit the snow six feet below like a diver punching water, making a neat hole up to her hips. As soon as she steadied herself, exhaustion hit her like an avalanche and she sank back on her bottom.

But she didn't dare sit long enough for her jeans to get wet. She twisted around to look at the mouth of the small cave behind her, under the ledge. The drifting snow had almost blocked it. Good. She scrambled toward the opening on her knees, then lay flat and scooted behind the drift into the pitch-black cave. She cringed farther back when she heard feet stamping up onto the cornice above.

Her pursuer shouted in Russian and his voice sounded enraged.

She fought to control her breathing, to keep it soundless. If he walked to the edge and shone his light down, he would see the mess she'd made in the snow below the cornice. But if her trick worked, he'd think her trail led the other way, into the trees.

The glare of his light fanned over the waterfall and onto the opposite bank of the creek. The Russian shouted something again, but right in the middle of his sentence, he stopped with a grunt.

After a heartbeat she heard a thump on the rock above her, then the whizzing of what had to be a second arrow.

Adam!

The Russian's flashlight dropped in the snow right in front of her, its beam pointing up.

She scrambled out and snatched it, fumbling with freezing fingers to find the switch. She backed into the cave and killed the light, knowing Adam couldn't use the binoculars if a halogen was glaring in the vicinity. Oh, God. Was she assisting him in murder?

Then the first shiver hit her.

Hypothermia.

Bundled in her heavy parka, she'd begun to sweat from exertion and fear. Bad. Dampness made hypothermia ten times worse. As she realized how much trouble she was in, her heart started to race again. She tried to be calm. She had to force herself not to panic, had to conserve her energy.

She unzipped the pocket of the parka and dug out her mittens, managing to get them on over scraped, shaking hands. She pulled her stocking cap down and her scarf up over her face. As long as she could perform simple motor activities...

But now what? She listened. And heard nothing except the rush of the waterfall and the notes of the tinkling river below, sounding strangely serene.

ADAM WAITED. At least he'd hit one of them—too large to be Toly Gradoff—on the rock ledge across the river...above Laura. Two down, one to go.

But the man had called out just before Adam's arrow struck, and if Adam's command of Russian served him, he'd told Gradoff that Laura had gone down toward the creek. Obviously he'd seen the patch of snow where she'd landed when she jumped off that cornice.

Adam had watched her pull that maneuver over the ledge. And he couldn't help admiring her courage and her quick thinking. She'd killed the blinding light, and maybe she'd be okay for now inside the small cave.

The snowmobile was parked on the opposite ridge, waiting for their trip down. *Come on, Gradoff.*

He adjusted the binoculars and waited. *Stay warm, Laura. Don't panic.*

GRADOFF STOPPED in his tracks, breathless. He took an inhaler from his pocket and sucked two quick puffs into his lungs. "That bitch," he wheezed aloud in Russian.

He took two more raking breaths, "We get him," he muttered. "I am sick of this crap."

"Iosif!" he bellowed out into the snowy air, then broke into a spate of coughing. No answer. He started back up the trail in the direction where he'd last heard Iosif's voice. When he came to the place where the woman had made the circular tracks in the snow, he realized she could have circled back. Then he saw Iosif.

LAURA HAD STARTED to worry about the bear.

She had been thinking positive thoughts, about how warm and protective the drifted snow was, about what a cozy...den this was.

When, exactly, did bears go into hibernation? It was late October. Could the sow be behind her now, asleep in this dark cave?

Laura inched the scarf down and inhaled a deep testing breath. The air under the ledge smelled piney.

She listened. Heard nothing. *Stop freaking yourself out. There's no bear. And you have two choices—sit here, or go out and face bullets.*

Laura closed her eyes and swallowed, tried not to think about the nightmare she was experiencing. The man she loved, the man who was the father of her baby, was systematically killing other human beings one by one.

But she didn't have long to think about it. The next thing she heard sounded like...breathing.

She was so shocked she stopped shivering while she held her breath and listened harder. Something in the darkness moved!

Laura bolted out of the cave and landed on all fours. She tumbled down the slope toward the river. Only a stand of small willows kept her from plunging into the frigid water.

No sooner had she caught her breath than she was bathed in blinding light.

"Come back up the bank on your hands and knees," Gradoff called from behind the light, "slowly."

FOR A SECOND the brightness of the halogen light blinded Adam. By the time he'd ripped the night-vision binoculars off and regained his vision, Laura was crawling up the bank in its glare.

In a split second of decisiveness, he tossed away the arrow tipped with the tranquilizer pod and reached into the quiver on his hip for the expandable head with the razor-sharp blades. He had to take out Gradoff before the guy got his hands on Laura again. One shot with this thing should do it. But he had to take that shot quickly before Laura got in the way. The angle of the light told him Gradoff stood in profile to him. He aimed directly at the darkness behind the light.

He heard Gradoff scream and suddenly the light flared skyward, hitting the snow, shining on Laura as she lost her footing and fell backward, sliding downhill headfirst. He heard her scream and the splash in the same instant.

He leaped off the boulder and bolted down the embankment on the opposite side of the river.

"Laura!" he yelled into the black torrent.

On the other side, a dark figure cursed and struggled to his knees in the glare of the fallen light, but Adam couldn't afford the luxury of stalking his prey.

He dived into the water.

For one instant of horror the icy water arrested all breath, all thought, all sensation.

He cried out when he came to the surface, terrified of what the crushing cold would do to Laura. To their baby. The river around him was a dark thundering mass that revealed nothing. No sign of life. No sign of Laura.

He fought the current for one mad instant, then pointed his legs out ahead of him and allowed himself to be swept along—toward her, he hoped.

He could hear the falls just ahead. *Please God*, he prayed, *don't let her go over*.

His boots bounced off rocks on all sides, then his feet bumped something looser. In the moonlight he caught a glimpse of the ribbons of hair swirling around her head as she drifted away.

He swam frantically to catch up to her, snatching at her red jacket in the dark current, but the instant he had her in his grip he felt the pull of the falls.

Together, they went over. Together, they went under.

Adam fought the force of the churning dark water with all his strength. He still had Laura in his grip, but the roiling water tumbled him in its disorienting darkness. His lungs burned, but he managed to stay calm and keep Laura with him, fighting to reach the surface. His head bobbed into the night air like a cork and he pulled Laura up as he gasped for breath.

His bad arm and shoulder burned with pain, but he kept his hold on her and kicked toward shore. The water was only deep in the center— he felt his boots touch bottom as soon as he told himself this. Despite the paralyzing cold, he managed to wrap his arms tightly around Laura and drag her onto shore, fueled by feverish determination.

When he got her up onto the bank, he laid her

in the snow and knelt over her, shivering. "Laura!" he cried, shaking her.

He turned her on her side as she started to cough and choke out water. Even though she started breathing, he delivered several quick breaths by mouth-to-mouth resuscitation, hoping the air in his lungs would warm her.

She came around enough to moan, "Adam."

He kissed her cold forehead. "Stay with me, sweetheart. We'll get you warm." His shoulder was on fire, his right arm felt numb, and his legs trembled with weakness. But with his last ounce of strength he gathered her up in his arms. She would die if anything happened to her—to *their*—baby. And he would die if anything happened to her.

CHAPTER EIGHTEEN

HIS ONLY THOUGHT of Gradoff was to hope that the man was dead or at least so injured he couldn't shoot at them. They'd come ashore far downstream, and the struggle back to the snowmobile was uphill and rocky. But Adam's legs felt stronger as he climbed. The exertion and the fact that he had Laura in his arms, alive, warmed him.

When he reached the snowmobile, he balanced her behind him on the seat and fired up the snowmobile. "Hold on, sweetheart, hold on." Her eyes were closed now and she was shivering so hard she could barely clutch his shoulders. He took her arms down and wrapped them around his waist.

Weaving through the trees, back over the narrow trail he'd forged on the way up, he made it to the clearing in a blur.

He braked the snowmobile and was shivering even harder by the time he carried her into the stone house. Inside he placed her on the bed and tucked the sleeping bag around her. She was shivering violently now.

From his supply box he grabbed a first-aid kit and dry towels. He ripped open four emergency chemical packs and snapped them, releasing their heat.

He sat her upright and started stripping off her wet clothing. When her upper body was naked, he pressed a chemical pack under each of her armpits and one under her chin. He put the fourth under his own left arm. Then he covered her upper body and started pulling off her wet boots and jeans.

When he'd gotten her completely out of the wet clothes, he dried her quickly with the towels, then tucked her into the sleeping bag.

Laura seemed at last to feel the effect of the warm packs. "G-Grad-doff…" she tried, but her teeth started chattering.

"I doubt he'll bother us."

Laura tried to sit up, still shaking so hard she could hardly speak, but this time she forced herself to finish the sentence. "H-how do you kn-know that?"

"Because I shot him with a steel-tipped expanding arrow just before you fell into the river." He wrapped a dry towel around her hair and tucked the down pillow up around her ears. "Now breathe deeply. You need the oxygen."

While he jerked off his wet outer clothes, Laura drew in a huge breath. Then another. The deep breathing calmed her and in a moment her shivering subsided somewhat. "Adam, y-you're wet, t-too."

"Not for long." He bent down and gave her a reassuring squeeze, then clumped over to the fireplace and knelt before it. He put in kindling, then snatched up the kerosene can from beside the camp stove and sprinkled the wood. She saw the glow of a match reflecting around his broad shoulders. When the wood burst into a roaring blaze, he began stripping off his thermals.

Laura watched his efficient movements, and she couldn't help the tears that came to her eyes. She loved this man. But what was to become of the two of them? Could she really make a life with a man who had done what Adam had done? Would she want her child to know what its father had done?

She tried not to think about the two dead men lying out there in the snow. She looked at the lifeless form near the door and closed her eyes.

When she opened them, he'd removed his thermals. "As soon as I make you some cocoa, I've got to go down to the big cabin—Toeless's cell phone is in the river—and call the authorities." He grabbed a towel and started drying himself. "Then I'll take the snowmobile back up and bring the other guy down here. We can't leave him out in the cold too long, or he'll die of hypothermia.''

Laura blinked. What was he saying? Hypothermia? "Aren't they already dead?" she whispered.

Adam froze with the towel stretched across his back. "What?"

Laura was confused. "Isn't that what you wanted—to kill them?"

"Kill?" he said as if dazed. "Is that what you thought?"

Laura nodded.

He dropped the towel and flattened his palms against the mantel over the fireplace, lowering his head and staring into the flames. His muscles looked massive, flexing and tensing in the orange glow. "Laura, the only time I wanted to kill someone was when Gradoff was about to get his hands on you."

She nodded again and started shivering again at the memory.

"I wouldn't mess up my life that way. Especially not now that I've found you."

"Oh, Adam."

"But we can talk about us later. Right now you need to drink something warm and sweet." He took the wool blanket off the couch and wrapped it snugly around his shoulders, then filled the tea kettle and crossed to the camp stove and lit a burner. He dug around in his cache for packets of hot chocolate.

While the water heated, he came back to the bed and sat down on the edge next to Laura. "Laura, listen. I've been unfair to you. I should have told you everything. But I...I just never imagined you'd be up here when I had to deal with them.''

A shudder passed through his body. He brushed her hair back from her forehead and studied her face sadly. "You believe me, don't you? I never planned to kill anyone. The smaller arrows I used had tips filled with a tranquilizer that immobilizes—but only temporarily. I only wanted to make sure they didn't escape this time. I want them to come to justice for what they did to Elizabeth and Anna. And I couldn't let them have the formula to use for their own gain. Do you understand?''

Tears filled Laura's eyes. She took a hand out of the sleeping bag and reached for him. "Oh, Adam, I should have known.''

He squeezed her cold fingers.

The sound of a four-wheel drive downshifting intruded. Laura panicked and clutched Adam's hand. "They're coming back!''

But Adam put two quieting fingers to her lips and shook his head.

Then a knock sounded at the door. He loosened her fingers and gently tucked her hand back under the sleeping bag. ''Gradoff wouldn't bother to knock, sweetheart,'' he said as he crossed the room.

He looked outside, then pulled the door open.

Laura stifled a yelp at the sight of a hulking man in a ski mask.

''Toeless.'' Adam said in exactly the same tone he'd used that first night when Elko arrived. ''Get your ass in here.''

Toeless slipped inside and Adam slammed the door against the cold.

''Just in time for cocoa,'' Adam said dryly.

Toeless smirked. ''What? No cookies?'' He jerked the ski mask off, adjusted his eye patch and narrowed his good eye at Adam. ''Don't get snotty with me, Perfessor. I drove up Sixteen Mile Creek Road like I was in the Grand Prix.'' He poked a thumb over his shoulder. ''Did you lose something?''

Adam peered into the dark outside the window. ''What the...?''

Toeless pressed his flashlight against the glass, aiming at something outside. ''Looks like a deer strapped across the hood like that, doesn't he?''

''It's Gradoff,'' Adam explained to Laura. ''Tied to the hood of Toeless's Land Rover.''

''With an arrow in his butt.'' Toeless winked

at her. "I couldn't exactly prop him up in the passenger seat, could I?" He shrugged. "The engine'll keep him warm for now."

Adam began charging around the room, gathering up dry clothes. "Where'd you capture him?"

"Capture? More like a rescue. He was struggling through a snowbank, sporting that arrow in his keister, screamin' in Russian about bleedin' to death. But if it weren't for old Toeless," he bared his teeth in a grin "—that little punk woulda froze to death before he bled to death."

"I don't want the bastard in here with Laura," Adam said.

So while Adam made Laura a mug of cocoa and quickly dressed, Toeless took Gradoff down to the main cabin to build a fire there. He'd also call the authorities.

When Adam heard the whine of Toeless's Land Rover returning up the path, he threw more logs on the fire.

"You stay warm." He crossed the room the Laura. "I've got to go help Toeless round up the other guy."

"What about him?" she looked at the inert form across the room.

"He'll be out for while, but we'll take him with us."

Adam sat on the bed and wrapped his arms

around her again, and at last she started to cry. "Oh, Adam. Is it over? Do you think it's finally over?" she murmured against his neck.

"For me it is," he said against her hair. "When I saw you fall into that water, I knew." He tilted her chin up and looked into her eyes. "Right at that instant I didn't care about Gradoff, the formula, or any of it. In that instant I had to let go of my need for vengeance in order to save you. And once I had you in my arms, I knew you're all that mattered to me. When Elizabeth and Anna died, I thought I could never love anyone again, but I was wrong, Laura. You see, there was something that I hadn't counted on."

"What was that?" she sniffed.

He studied her face for a moment before he spoke. "You."

She turned her face up to his as a flood of emotions almost too rich to bear coursed through her.

"Kiss me, Adam Scott or Adam Schneider or whatever your name is, because I'm the woman who loves you. The woman who's going to have your baby."

They were both still shivering, but the warmth of the kiss they shared calmed their trembling.

In fact, Adam thought as he savored Laura's sweet mouth, this woman's kisses warmed him in a way that nothing else on the face of the earth ever could.

EPILOGUE

FRINGES OF GREEN peeked around the last patches of snow, shyly offering the warm promise of spring.

Laura stood at the tall window in the dining room of her little house in Kalispell, holding the lace curtain aside, admiring Adam and Doc's handiwork, and feeling as if she might overflow with happiness at any second.

Tiny white lights spiraled up the tree trunks, across the gate and around the newel posts beside the porch steps, ready to be lit just before the guests arrived tonight. Sylvia Summers had trimmed the front door with a huge wreath of dried wildflowers and a big baby-boy-blue ribbon.

At first Adam had wanted to rent the entire Kalispell Grand Hotel for the baby shower.

Of course, they could have held the party up at the stone house or even the big cabin. But Laura didn't want her friends to have to drive up Sixteen Mile Creek Road.

And Katherine and Doc, the darlings, had offered to have it at their house, but again, there was the problem of that awful road.

Reverend Green, when he heard a baby shower was being planned, said why not have it at the church meeting hall, where Laura and Adam had been married. Laura joked that he must have forgiven them for the unconventional wedding: a shaggy old dog in attendance and "Itsy-Bitsy Spider" as prelude music.

In the end Laura had decided to hold the shower back at her little house in Kalispell. "It's my own special place, and I want to have one last celebration there," she told Adam.

"Anything you want, sweetheart."

That was what he always said.

What she wanted was to keep it simple. A dozen or so friends from Mountain Home Health Care and her church, Doc and Katherine, Toeless, Adam's mom and sisters, and of course Morton.

Laura fogged the window with her breath and traced a tiny heart on the pane with her finger.

Yesterday had been such a sad sweet day. A day of closure, a day of goodbyes. Tomorrow, Adam and Toeless would be moving the last of Laura's homey antiques up to the cabin on Sixteen Mile Creek. The big cabin wouldn't be bare anymore. Then she would sign this house over.

It would become the Kalispell Children's Center—a nursery and preschool to be run by the church.

Laura knew their visits to Sixteen Mile Creek would become less frequent with a baby in tow. It was a long trip up here from Southern California, where they had started their new life. They'd decided to make their permanent home there, near Adam's family. Being close to Adam's mother and his sisters was important to Laura. The women had accepted her wholeheartedly and were eagerly awaiting the arrival of the newest member of the family.

Several friends from church and Mountain Home Health had already dropped by yesterday, anxious to visit with Laura. This afternoon, some of the ladies brought special goodies to spice up tonight's simple fare of cake and punch.

Out of the corner of her eye Laura saw Katherine slap Doc's fingers away from a tin of homemade cookies.

"There's more food here than the whole town can eat in a week," he protested.

Laura had to agree as she surveyed the treats covering every surface of her cozy dining room. "Well, I suppose this is also a goodbye party."

Katherine walked over to Laura, beside the window.

Laura turned and smiled, then shook her head.

"More like a smorgasbord than a baby shower, isn't it?"

Laura's whole life felt like that these days. An endless feast. Adam loved to spoil her and she loved to let him. She reached up and touched the one-carat diamond earrings he'd given her as a wedding gift.

Laura smiled. She had been able to do her share of giving, too. This house, for example. She hoped to find other wonderful ways to share their wealth. Amazing that Stuart hadn't ever mentioned the Dallas property again. Laura had contacted the lawyers and signed the deed on her own.

"Guess he read the newspapers and didn't want an arrow in his butt," Toeless had joked.

"I believe you're right, *Jerome,*" Laura had teased.

Toeless actually blushed. "I told that reporter my name was Toeless."

Laura had saved all the articles, of course. Hidden away, where Adam wouldn't have to read them, but someday, she would show them to their child so he could see how incredibly brave his father was. Laura had pored over the stories so often she practically had them memorized.

Three Russian émigrés, wanted for more than a year on charges of homicide in the deaths of a local woman and her child, were taken into custody yesterday in northwestern Montana.

The husband and father of the victims, Adam Schneider, and logger Jerome Elko handed the suspects over to authorities in the small town of Libby after apprehending the men in a remote area of the Kootenai National Forest.

Police said one of the suspects, suffering from a severe arrow wound to the buttocks, remains hospitalized. The other two, suffering from minor wounds and mild aftereffects from tranquilizing arrows, are confined to the Lincoln County jail.

It all seemed so unreal, so long ago, when now Adam and Laura couldn't seem to stem the flow of happiness and riches into their lives. Laura smiled. That was because Adam couldn't seem to stem his flow of bigger, more creative ideas.

After he donated the prototypes to a major university, which agreed to develop the medicine under strict safety guidelines, he started to work on his next project. Adam's lawyers stipulated that his portion of the income from the nano-explosive drug go to Doc and Katherine, with a special request that they take care of Morton, who seemed to have moved in with them.

"Despite all this party food—" Katherine touched Laura's shoulder and interrupted her reminiscing "—I think you'd better come and have a decent meal first." She tugged at Laura's elbow. "Come. I made lentil soup."

Laura smiled. Katherine and her soups. And her fussing.

"Do you know where Adam went?" she asked Doc and Katherine as they seated themselves at the little table in the kitchen.

"I think he had an errand," Doc answered cryptically.

"He'll be back in plenty of time for the shower," Katherine said.

But Doc had turned on the twinkling lights out front and the guests had started to arrive, and still there was no sign of Adam. Laura tried not to worry, but it was so unlike Adam to be late.

She was standing, with her hands tucked around her big belly, laughing with one of Adam's sisters, when he came bursting in the front door.

The room fell silent.

"Well, Adam. There you are," Katherine said softly.

"And it's certainly not hard to guess where you've been," his mother added cheerfully.

Everyone in the room chuckled.

Adam stepped forward, his gaze fixed on Laura, full of love. He gave her one of his crooked grins.

"Sorry I'm late." He held his gift out to his wife. "I drove up to our meadow to get these. I got started picking and couldn't stop. They're absolutely glorious this year."

"Oh, Adam," Laura breathed, "wildflowers. And my favorite ones."

She reached out to her husband, taking an enormous basket overflowing with freshly picked bitterroot and butter-and-eggs. It was a simple gift for this special occasion, but for Laura, there could have been none finer. And besides, Adam had already given her the finest gifts a man could give a woman. His care. His love. His healed heart.

Inside her, the baby boy kicked, and Laura closed her eyes. Oh, yes, Adam Scott had already given her the very finest gift.

Back by popular demand are

DEBBIE MACOMBER's

Hard Luck, Alaska, is a
town that needs women!
And the O'Halloran brothers
are just the fellows
to fly them in.

Starting in March 2000 this beloved series returns
in special 2-in-1 collector's editions:

MAIL-ORDER MARRIAGES, featuring
Brides for Brothers and *The Marriage Risk*
On sale March 2000

FAMILY MEN, featuring
Daddy's Little Helper and *Because of the Baby*
On sale July 2000

THE LAST TWO BACHELORS, featuring
Falling for Him and *Ending in Marriage*
On sale August 2000

Collect and enjoy each MIDNIGHT SONS story!

Available at your favorite retail outlet.

She's stolen his heart, but should she be trusted?

CANDACE CAMP

Lord Thorpe's new American business partner, Alexandra Ward, is beautiful, outspoken *and* the perfect image of a woman long thought dead. Her appearance on Thorpe's arm sends shock rippling through society, arouses hushed whispers in the night. Is she a schemer in search of a dead woman's fortune, or an innocent caught up in circumstances she doesn't understand?

Someone knows the truth, someone who doesn't want Alexandra to learn too much. Only Lord Thorpe can help her—if he can overcome his own suspicions. But even if he does, at what price?

A STOLEN HEART

*On sale mid-March 2000
wherever paperbacks are sold!*

HEART OF THE WEST

Every Man Has His Price!

Lost Springs Ranch was famous for turning young mavericks into good men. So word that the ranch was in financial trouble sent a herd of loyal bachelors stampeding back to Wyoming to put themselves on the auction block!

HARLEQUIN®
Makes any time special ™

Visit us at www.romance.net

PHHOWGEN